memories of

KAOS

To a great man who
also happens to be a great
chef.

[signature]

2-16-08

memories of

KAOS

The Lost Sons of God

a novel

Bradford D. Acton

TATE PUBLISHING *& Enterprises*

Published by Tate Publishing & Enterprises, LLC
127 E. Trade Center Terrace | Mustang, Oklahoma 73064 USA
1.888.361.9473 | www.tatepublishing.com

Tate Publishing is committed to excellence in the publishing industry. The company reflects the philosophy established by the founders, based on Psalms 68:11,
"The Lord gave the word and great was the company of those who published it."

Book design copyright © 2007 by Tate Publishing, LLC. All rights reserved.
Cover design by Lindsay Behrens
Interior design by Jennifer Redden

Published in the United States of America

ISBN: 978-1-60247-491-8
07.06.12

To my encouragement, my inspiration, and my best friend. The only angel I have ever known.

For you, Em. Always.

ACKNOWLEDGMENTS

The writing of *Memories of Kaos* revealed to me that no book ever came about because of an author's individual effort. Many individuals are responsible, directly and indirectly, for the completion of this work. The following list contains only a fraction of the number I am able to thank:

My parents, Don and Kathy, for believing in me from the start, when I 'read' before I knew how.

My wife, Emily, to whom this book is dedicated, for encouraging a husband lost in his doubt.

My brothers, Brook and Branch, who taught me the value of combat.

Daniel Milton, a friend who believed in my story when I felt I no longer could.

Andrew Louderback, for editing the embarrassment I called a 'draft.'

Nathan Lucy, for telling me authors can actually make it in this world.

Teachers, friends, and family to whom I owe all that I am.

The people at Tate Publishing, who made my dream a reality when many others said it was impossible.

Our Heavenly Father, for giving my tired hands the strength to pen this story. This book is now in His hands, and to whomever it goes, may they see Him in the reading as I saw Him in the writing.

CONTENTS

FOREWORD

Bradford D. Acton has written a gripping saga of deceit, dishonor, and rebellion—and of faithfulness, integrity, and courage. Or, as Kaos, (the central character in the story) says in the Prologue: "No, this is no story of peace. It is one of life and death, of hope and despair, of faith and character."

It is all of this—and more. Acton writes of Lucifer's rebellion in Heaven, and in the process raises questions of the greatest magnitude. If God—as He claims in His Word—is Sovereign, then how does a rebellion against Him become possible? If He is Good, then why does He allow evil to exist at all? If—as He claims—He is faithful to those who commit themselves to Him, then how can He allow them so often to suffer, and endure such pain, for so long, in their lives?

Acton writes with eloquence and great skill, drawing the reader into his vivid description of evil's war against good, into that realm of tortuous decisions people must make who find themselves in moments of great temptation and great peril.

This is a splendid beginning of what we hope will be a long writing career.

Peter Reese Doyle, Th.D

PROLOGUE

"If this was to be a story of peace, I could have crafted volumes on nothing more than the genesis of Time itself. I remember when I believed what we established in the beginning would uphold itself for eternity, but our hopes were destroyed in what was wrought even before Time began.

"Only two of your race knew perfection, while my entire kind flourished in untainted existence. I knew peace; you only dream of it. I have witnessed true love as it was meant for you, but you can only grasp at the mimicry of what once was pure. I walked the borders of heaven and sat amidst the infant stars, the very same you long for as you gaze at their evanescent reminders, dying in the sky. None of my kind knew war, nor strife, nor pain. My brothers and I dwelled in structured harmony, until we, as did your kind, fell from our appointed places.

"The murmurs of rebellion began long before I was cursed to witness the destruction of those I had been created to love. Some had grown jealous of Man, the Father's newest undertaking. The usurpers whispered in secret that He had gone so far as to favor them over us, the very first of His Creation. Thus, envy became our first sin.

"The plot of the rebellious continued to spread, yet my Father did nothing. In those times I bore witness to much I wish forgotten. I knew wrath. I witnessed grief. I held the dying. I guarded the weak. I walked with the strong. I wept for peace as I warred with those I once knew as brothers.

"No, this is no story of peace. It is one of life and death, of hope and despair, of faith and cowardice. It will show you the depths of supernatural emotion, and you will be repeatedly reminded of your own mortality. As your own life lengthens and fades, remember my words and the history of eternity past so you will be prepared for the ages to come. I forever regret that this is a broken story, a forgotten story, and as such, it must and can only be, an angel's story."

I

"Kaos."

My name called me from my meditations as I turned. The dearest
of my brothers approached from the Gates. Visitors rarely came
out past the portal, even though I never wandered far from the
gates. The soft, glowing hue of my eyes temporarily shuttered as I
blinked and turned back towards my previous view of the Abyss.

"You are easy to find, my friend."

Novation. Everything he is reminds me of all we would lose.
His laughter never hid itself and his eyes sparked with compassion.
His faithfulness served as an example of what should have been,
what we should have been.

"Hello, brother. I only try to ensure my availability to those
who would readily take advantage of my time, not excluding you,"
I joked.

My friend's smile temporarily graced the ground before his face
became slowly devoid of humor. We grew silent for a few, fleeting
moments; our eyes scanning the terrible beauty of the chaos from

which we came, before Novation spoke again. "The old days are gone, Kaos. Trust is dead, and all of the hosts whisper secrets in shadows."

"Why do you think the days have grown different?"

"The rumors have not stopped, Kaos, as we all thought they would. I am beginning to think they never will, and it fills me with an emotion I have never experienced. It is as if I am anxious, but in a darker sense. I do not know a word to communicate it to you." Novation's eyes slowly closed as he sat beside me.

I continued to quietly gaze across the border of Zion. I had taken no stock in the rumors. If our Father wished them silenced, He would command it to be so. Yet, He was the one that remained silent. Council had once been given freely to any who sought Him out, but as of late, the Throne remained closed to most.

"Have you heard the most recent murmurings, Kaos?"

I disliked rhetorical questions. It always seemed as if the one who asked took pride or feared the information they possessed. In my friend's case, I knew that he was simply intimidated by what the answer implied.

"You know I have, brother, but whether I've chosen to believe what I've heard is the dilemma I share with the rest of our kind."

I turned again to the expanse of light-filled nothingness that encircled the end of order. Upon a deeper look, one could ascertain that it was not simply an expanse or rift, but a tear in the very fabric of Creation. At other times you could almost feel a connection, a bond, with that untouched madness, the chaos from which we came when called by the Father, according to His Will.

"It's almost beautiful."

"You mean sublime."

"Regardless of one or the other, your namesake frightens me."

"It cannot *be* here, Novation. There is no chaos to fear in this place."

His solemn gaze scanned back and forth over the frothing colors, caught in a perpetual dance, storming against itself on its edge of existence.

"I do not fear that, Kaos, but I tremble to think if any of that remains in us, hidden deep, and well, behind everything we built."

"We are new, brother. There is nothing of the old self in us."

"So you say, but you have refused to see what I have seen. There is madness in the hosts, and it will spread. The rumors are…"

"Just that, rumors. They will die out, and so will your fears. Have faith."

"It is not my faith I came to accredit. You show apathy in the face of annihilation, displaying a calm that is vanishing from this land. I wonder if it is foolishness, or faith, as you claim," Novation challenged.

"When was their last gathering? They are silent, hiding in their own lies. If they rose up, all would be crushed, especially these Lessers bulking their ranks."

"There is another meeting to be called, Kaos. I heard through Origin that it is to be held in Sardis."

"Sardis? Such a public place? When the Lords Mel'akim find them out they will be destroyed." I often grew weary of the murmurings that came from our weaker brothers. Concern had grown that our Father worked beyond the realms of Zion, that He crafted anew, things still unknown to us. I never cared for the rumors. If my maker had spread His Creation out into the Abyss and beyond, I had no say in the matter. He was my Sovereign.

Novation's eyes slowly closed as a shy breath blew from his lips, "The Lords will do nothing in light of who leads the next gathering. You don't know, do you?"

I did not know. "Why does it matter? If you have not noticed, none of the Chief Princes have ever attended, nor have the Archangels. The stirrings between our brethren will grow old and—"

"The Son of Light, Kaos. Our *Captain*."

I stood silent for several seconds. That could not be. If the Angel of Hosts held this meeting, then the situation had grown far worse than I anticipated. "Novation, you must be wrong. If he really is behind all this, it could, it could lead to—I know not what it means, but I…"

"I know, I know, Kaos. That is why I came to find you. I did not know what else to do." Novation slowly stood, his glowing robes falling into place around his feet as he turned to go. I believe that was the first time I truly studied my friend. The soft, green glow of his eyes pulsed in harmony with the hue of his light green skin. Essence given to him at Creation emanated from the mass of lights that lay tangled atop his head. His kind eyes were set in a soft face that seemed aflame with light.

"Are you sure the Bright One will be there?" My own rhetorical question proved the same in me as it had in my friend earlier. I was afraid.

"Yes, I am sure. You will be summoned. You are one of the Chosen. When you are, it remains to you whether to go or stay." I heard him sigh beside me as he gracefully stood. "Find your faith, Kaos. Soon it will be too late. They will dethrone Jehovah." With that, Novation began gliding back to the Gates.

"Where will you go, if not to the meeting?" I ventured.

Novation slowly turned as his eyes steadily rose to meet mine. "I do not know what will happen, Kaos, but if this tainted communion continues to grow there will be a struggle. I do not know how it will be orchestrated, but there will be a clash. When that comes to pass I wish to be found by the doors of my Father's Throne. That is where I will wait, until I receive better counseling."

"And if it does lead to rebellion, Novation? What will you do then?"

"If they bring their fight to the Lord who made me and knows me then I will make my stand, for what it is worth, at the stairs of the Throne." He began to turn and go, but he asked one more question I have always remembered. "Where will you stand, Kaos?"

"I do not know, Novation. If the Second is holding the meeting, then there may be hidden truths we do not know." My friend's eyes sank as I spoke. "But I will never go so far as to fight against our Creator, brother. I wish only to hear what the Second to our God knows."

"You may be demanded of a decision far earlier than you have the time to plot its possible course. I will come to you, Kaos, or else, if all occurs as it should, I would hope you still come to me."

All was madness in my mind that day. Until that point I always considered the rebellion as nothing more than a pathetic plot conjured up by those in lower positions, jealous of those esteemed to higher services. If the Captain, however, the Morning Star, Lucifer, the Guardian himself lay behind these plots, what did that imply? He knew no cause for jealousy. He saw God in the depths of His midst. If nothing else, the lower brothers would be jealous of him, not vice versa.

I decided to follow Novation back inside the gates, thinking over what I'd heard. None of it made sense, unless Lucifer knew something we did not. Perhaps there was more to this "Man" than our Father revealed. He had no need to replace us, or so we wagered. For now, I could only wait for the summons, and then decisions would be made, mine amongst the least of them, or so I thought.

II

"I looked up and there before me was a man dressed in linen, with a belt of the finest gold around his waist. His body was like chrysolite, his face like lightning, his eyes like flaming torches, his arms and legs like the gleam of burnished bronze, and his voice like the sound of a multitude."

-Daniel 10:5–6-

The path back towards the gate glimmered as I paced behind Novation. "Maybe nothing will come from this."

"You know something will come from this, Kaos. We are only too scared to think of what that something might be."

Off to our right, a deep gorge ringed a mountain range bearing off ahead and behind us. Its peaks glistened in radiance while far below in the gorge the deep thunder of moving water echoed up the walls. "Have you ever wondered why He made us, Kaos?"

It was a familiar question. We knew what He made us for, and we knew how He made us, but none of us knew why He made us. "I used to think it was solely for worship, for His own glory, or for our pleasure. Things change, however. I'm not sure anymore."

"I look at these things around us. I see power. I see grace and majesty. These things were made by Him to demonstrate Himself; they had to have been. If the Father is wholly good and simultaneously omnipotent, He could not have helped but portray His qualities throughout His work."

"So what does that say of us, then?"

"It means we are more than tools and mere representations of a God who desires relationship with His Creation. What we are exactly, however, I do not know."

We walked further down the path, occasionally falling into silence as we tried to forget our problems. We would laugh, and Novation even sang when the mountains from before disappeared behind a turn in the road. I just smiled when he sang and pondered while he was quiet. The path turned several more times, exposing vast plots of land reaching out into the horizon.

"No matter what, little brother, take care of yourself. Don't do anything crazy, and stay hidden from the others until it settles down."

He smiled. "Kaos, all will happen as it should, and when all these things are over, I'll reach back into the days before this day and remember when we never had to worry. No matter what happens, you can always find me there."

"This is madness, and if it were not for Lucifer, I would dismiss it all as lies."

"Yet you believe there must be some truth to his claims of a deception," he pressed.

"There is truth in all things to some degree. To what we can only guess. I know something is going to happen, but I do not know how it will occur. Satan will put his case before the Father and I pray mercy upon all of us when he does."

"Yes—mercy."

We wandered the Border for some time, wondering what destruction these revealed implications would bring to pass. As my thoughts tossed me into deeper turmoil, the summons came for me. It ran like a trembling vibration up the center of my back, eventually surging within my senses and informing me where to report. I could have resisted. I could have fled temptation had I known what temptation was.

High above the landscape, clouds formed, coalesced, and then disintegrated in an airy death, fading only long enough for a second cloud to form. Behind, a breeze whispered over me. In the sky, order and chaos molded with the other, pulsing, moving, and swaying in rhythm as lightning riddled the sky between the clouds. Fears again, always fear, welling within me, showing me where to jump, where to flee, out into that, out into nothing.

Again the breeze came, calling me back to where I belonged. I can not remember much of the beginning—before all this. In quiet moments, when all of time seemed to die for a moment in itself, I try to remember where I came from, and where He found me. It always came in dreams, hidden in sleep, when my mind tried to forget, and then I remembered.

I could not leave my Father.

Wings of pure ethereal energy sprang from my back then slowly solidified. "I'll come back, little brother. They summon me."

"Remember yourself, Kaos. Many things we forget, but always remember yourself. I'll be waiting for you."

I launched into the air of my Father's Kingdom and raced to the Hall of Sardis. Far below me the landscape our Lord once sculpted flashed by so fast I forgot to wonder whether I would see these skies after today. Every plain, every rolling hill, the colors that reflected the nature of God dancing over them all, slid beneath me, reminding me of their Maker, leaving me without excuse aside from their aesthetic implications of the divine.

Sardis soon rose before me, coming into view as I plotted my course in my mind. Tall, looming towers cornered the vast expanse situated between them all. A domed, golden roof gleamed in the light of day and slightly blinded me as I fell through the clouds.

Monolithic doors stood closed before me. Their vast dimensions muted whatever took place inside so I strode slowly toward them along with others that arrived alongside me. The portal opened as we approached, gliding noiselessly closed as our group made its way inside, and then I saw the masses. Countless as the stars, all were crowding the area that had been previously used for the gathering of the Hosts before worship. At least a third of the hosts were already gathered.

I looked for no one in particular. I knew many of them by name. My senses guided my eyes towards Origen, being the one who sent the summons, as he concentrated in the calling forth of every chosen brother from within the borders of Zion. His eyes sat unseeing, glazed over in his efforts.

I stepped forward into the ocean of my brothers, walking over polished marble floors as lamp stands flickered off to my left and right. Shadows moved over the walls as light flowed over our gathering. Dark stones caught the light and threw them around us. Few moved out in the hall between the columns, and neither did I, until I spotted Solomyn.

He and I once wandered and explored the depths of heaven when all was new and unknown. I always remember him as a true brother of mine, a brother of blood, of life, and of death. Solomyn was given the ability to decipher the riddles of Creation. He possessed unparalleled wisdom, being able to interpret the meanings of the landscape, the messages encrypted in the very foundations of the plains, valleys, and mountains of our world. If anyone could be trusted in our world it would have to be Solomyn.

My eyes flamed quickly as I approached my old friend. His bright yellow eyes flared in recognition when they fell upon me, and his lightning-hued face split into a knowing smile as I came closer. A soft glow shimmered from his wise visage. I suspected I could trust his wisdom. His innocent smile faded as I alighted next to him. We embraced quickly, but there was no joy within our action. The gravity of our present circumstances hushed the pleasure in seeing the other.

"Hello, Kaos."

"Brother."

He gazed out into the masses, blinking intermittently as his eyes scanned back to me. "Who would have known this time would ever come? Of course, if I had any foresight at all, one would think I could have perceived the greatest deception of our time." His words comforted me.

"I hope you can help me, old friend. We both know the gifts given me do not include the discernment so given to you. From what you say it would appear that you view this meeting as what I feared it to be."

"What is it, exactly, that you fear?" His eyes gleamed with genuine concern.

"The rumors, Solomyn. How can they be true? This is madness. If Yahweh discovers us, all will be turned to ruin, and I do not understand how Lucifer can justify whatever claims he seeks to make. He is a deceiver. There can be no other answer."

"No, dear Kaos. The deception does not lie on the part of our High Lord Prince. What? Would you doubt the word of the Second? He has no cause, no prize to attain. He has all that can be offered from the Mount of God, yet He insists on our need to arise."

My friend's words shook me to the core of whom I was and who I had been, compelling me into a state of careless confusion. In such a short time, the rumors of the Least had arisen and taken captive the wisest of our brothers. Again, the fear rose up within me.

"You side with *Lucifer?* But what does he mean to do? He cannot overthrow the Throne of God. And what would that achieve? Why fight what is unconquerable? It is foolishness!" My faith quivered under my fears.

"Kaos, do you not know how our 'Father' has portended to further His Creation?"I only stared into his eyes as I felt the fires in my own flicker and quiver in disbelief. My legs shook in rhythm to the fevered flash of my eyes. "He plans to Shape again."

The Hall slowly filled as the torrent of voices reverberated from the arched heights of Sardis. "It cannot be true. *We* are His love. It was *us* He crafted first. How could He go behind the promises He cast for us and shape a second race? What could they give Him that we cannot?"

"Old friend, it is not as simple as all that. Our Father never saw it as part of His plan to reveal that plan to us. We sit in the dark as He wields his hand over chaos even now, crafting what He knows would bring calamity upon His first Kingdom. He operates in secret to hide the force He is shaping."

"Force?"

"A force by which to drive previous imperfection from His presence. A force by which to attain the perfection that, apparently, has not been found in us. Why else would he hold a second creation if not to remove the blemishes of the first?"

Shock hissed through my clenched teeth. "So, we are to be replaced?"

Compassion and resolute anger filled my friend's enlightened eyes. "No, my dear friend. We are to be destroyed."

"No. Solomyn…cannot be true. We are for His glory! Why would He wish to destroy that which was formed to bring Him pleasure?" My confusion felt shackled with grief and wrath. I turned quickly from my brother, unable to cope with what he proposed.

"Look around, Kaos. This is the end of an old way, and our new beginning." I considered those gathered around me, realizing they came here not for answers, but for excuses. I came for help, they came for revenge. I did not belong. "Why does this trouble you? It should not, must not. You are not alone in this. He has betrayed us, Kaos. He has betrayed you."

"Solomyn, I… This is not as it seems. It cannot be. Why are you here?"

"Because I desire to expose lies. This is why I was made. The pursuit of truth, and now I will use those gifts to hold my maker accountable to Truth itself."

"Yet did not our Maker create Truth? Or do you suppose Truth pre-existed the Father Himself?"

"I know not what was, only what is, and the actions of our God betray the Truth I uphold above all else."

"What if it is not the Father who lies, but His servants, perhaps for reasons we cannot know."

"Then I am damned for doing what I was made to do."

"Then it is pride keeping you here, Solomyn, and if you persist in this thought then make no mistake, God will receive His glory, whether you give it freely or not."

"Kaos, my friend, do not be a fool. I was made for this!"

"Perhaps, then, I was made for faith."

Solomyn's cries faded as I strode towards the doors, readying the Essence within me to bring forth my wings. Before I could ascend, however, a voice that resonated with the power of a multitude shot from the forefront of the gathering.

"Children of Zion and of God! Hear Me!"

My being shook with the power of our High Lord's voice. The wings I began to form recoiled with whip-like thunder, lashing back into my body. Here was the Second, and upon his words pivoted the future of us all. He stood adorned in a robe that knew no color and yet possessed all color. The perfection of his beauty compelled ours to fade, and as his voice rumbled and rolled through the Hall his thoughts became our thoughts. His Will, our Will.

Explosive thunders and cavernous echoes resounded within

Sardis; all of my brothers cowered as they listened to the Chief Prince. He instantly confirmed the rumors that still whispered through the hall. There was indeed to be a new creation, a Second Creation, for the Father was not fulfilled by what He made in the First. The Lord of the Hosts warned the Legions of what would arise from this second race.

"They will overtake the shortcomings that allowed all of us to fail. Where our weaknesses blinded the eyes of God and where our failures stilled His love, this race will thrive. His pleasure will be found in them, and His glory will be fulfilled by a grace given them yet denied to us. Once they have set their place in creation, our "Father" will use them to wipe away the scars of our faults. We will be *destroyed!*"

His words continued to rain down terror amongst my brothers and friends. More and more of them slowly bowed their heads with eyes closed in confusion and grief. When their eyes rose again they flashed in anger and wrath. At the time I had never seen emotions such as these manifested in the faces of my brothers. As the horror of seeing them stilled my steps I could only turn and listen to the words of our Lord.

"If we give Him the time, it will be too late. We must act. Now stands the hour of our eternity. The lies of the Father have sickened my ears, thus, I have come to drive you from His deception!"

"But how will we fight? We have no means by which to stop Him!"

The still small voice in the crowd seemed no more than a whisper. Few could discern what had been questioned, so Lucifer repeated his question to the masses, still unchecked, even by the interruption. Smooth, calm, yet full of vehement passion he followed his speech with the plan for Heaven's vindication.

"At the appropriate time, you will be given the means to fight.

Your very Essence that He called forth for you will be used against Him. If you but follow my lead, I will show you the way!"

I began walking to the edge of the crowd. Glancing back I saw Solomyn transfixed by the words of the Second. He never noticed me go. I made it to an outcropping that reached close to the ground along the borders of the hall. The tumult within Sardis grew as the lord of our hosts deliberated the plans for his rebellion. Soon, the power in the place became overbearing, almost intolerable. I felt myself becoming unraveled. If I had not fled at that very moment I fear what took place at the gathering would have overcome me. My faltering legs carried me for a short distance before I settled close to the doors, preparing to run at my next opportunity.

As a loud roar shook the hall I dashed towards the doors. I do not doubt the Second saw them open, but their movement went unnoticed amidst the thunder of the legions. Before the portal closed and as I took flight, the thunder of our Captain's voice chased me on the winds, and I heard Novation's words echoing towards the heavens, "*Where will you stand?!*"

I could not think. My eyes remained fixed ahead as my mind drove me towards the throne of my Father. So much needed to happen before I could decide my fate in what was now, it seemed, imminent. I could never fight the very Father that had called me forth, nor could I ignore the warnings of His Second. I chose to wait, subjecting myself to the perils of damnation, seeking to justify my cowardice as wisdom. Because of this I decided to stand by that day and behold the beginnings of damnation, and for my cowardice I have never forgotten the sorrows of that age, existing forever within the cruelty of our lamentations.

III

"And there was war in heaven…"

-Revelation 12:7-

There remained so much I could not comprehend. The likely promise of our destruction gripped me with terror as I coped with the notion of annihilation. There are some things worse than death I came to find. We were blind. We never wanted power or authority. We only craved acceptance, devotion, and love, the same love we lived to give back to the one who shaped us, molded us into His reality, but the Father now sat hidden in rumors that proposed notions of a new project, a second shaping. By these means He would replace us, and that would not do.

Upon this threat I soared. The citadel of the Almighty rose into view as I roared over the blur of the Kingdom. Shimmers of pale, powerful light sparked and slid from my wings as I flew. Flames burned out from my eyes, sliding over my face as Essence propelled me, allowing me no time to weep for which now seemed inexorable.

Neighbored to the Mount of God sat a small rise upon which I alighted. My wings faded, shrank, and slowly withdrew from where they had sprung. Below, the wide terrace merged into broad, marble steps that descended down to the earth. Jagged rock formations formed a narrow path unto the stairs at their base. This entry wound fifty paces or so out into the plains where the rocks disappeared into the rolling grasslands, shimmering in prismatic hues across its deep expanse. The citadel itself sat couched amongst sheer rock faces that clawed their way into the sky; none of them stood near as tall as the central spire itself, which tore a glorious wound through the middle of the heavens.

Embedded deep into the base of each column, sat a single, large stone. For each base there glowed a different color, and around each one a soft flame coiled and licked along its edges. The tender flames flowed over the lower halves of the columns forming a mirage of prismatic light that shown out onto the surrounding terrain.

I have forgotten for how I long I waited. I could make no decisions; I only sat, pondering the ways in which the end could come, trying to forget the nature of deceit while convincing myself of the possibility that I still served a good God.

A rising spire that reached out into the upper planes of heaven roofed the towering pillars and columns adorning the outer walls of the palace. Underneath the roof and within the walls laid the Throne, the mercy seat of God. Whether He knew of the rebellion or not, I could only guess. If He had lied to us so far, then nothing would have kept Him from lying about His power and omniscience as well. Up until now, we had been mere pawns, but if the rumors were true then these pawns would soon hold sway over the very ways of God Himself.

I meditated for a time until I was stirred by a small tremor in the back of my mind. It resembled a summons yet differed in some unnoticeable way. The Light of our God still issued from the Palace, but no one was to be seen. I was alone.

The pressure I felt deep in my mind directed my eyes over the endless plains that stretched away from the gates of the citadel.

From what seemed leagues away, a faint thunder grew beneath a cloudless sky. Then I saw them. A dark, shifting mass rumbled nearer and nearer. Soon after, I could no longer see the plains due to the army that covered them. My brothers, every one that stayed behind at Sardis, now marched ceaselessly over the expanse that bordered the capitol of Zion.

Awestruck, I remained unmoving as creation's first army thundered still closer. Never before had the hosts appeared as such. Now, they were the focal point. They were the power at hand and the force to behold. For a moment, I forgot any fear I once had for the Father. The fear again, rising, ever rising. I feared them. I feared the hosts, my brothers, as they came closer, marshaled for war.

Endless, countless, the Legions marched closer, surrounded in their own power, encompassed in their own glory. They needed no God; they became their own. With Zion as its prey, the thing my brothers had become closed in. I stood trembling on the mount, with nothing to defend myself from the horrors of what I witnessed.

As they spread over a once perfect creation I pressed myself to the hilltop, slitting my glowing eyes and gazing at the head of the endless columns. There, at the front, stood the Chief Prince of Heaven. The Bright One stood enveloped in brilliant radiance. His flaming eyes sent twin fires peaking above his head, while his six ethereal wings unfolded and flexed over the ranks immediately behind him. His long, shimmering white hair danced and swayed with energy while lightning sparked from his face and fizzled around him. He was in a state of power, force, and wrath.

The ranks ceased their approach only a short distance from the gates of the palace. Silence reigned as I peered from my post above. They stood still for a time, before the Second turned, observed his army, and slowly stalked back and forth in front of his officers. Several of the Chief Princes stood behind him, but in a humble state that was in no way comparable to the image their lord now gloriously displayed. They stood immediately behind the Second, but aside from their station, which I already knew, nothing else of their appearance hinted at the power they wielded. All were silent and calm as Satan roamed before his ranks, urging certain orders upon his officers, making periodical glances from the great doors back to his hosts.

I grew anxious on the mount, unsure of their lack of action. Lucifer soon stopped his pacing, however, and turned toward the temple, his colorless robe contradicting itself in a myriad of colors and mirages that changed and swirled as he moved.

Until that time, no being, no force, no power, had ever challenged the Almighty. No one dared confront the crafter of chaos, the Father of Time. He was I AM, and we were His subjects. Loved and upheld subjects, yet subjects just the same, and it was only a matter of time before the proudest among us would try to subjugate the subjugator. In a fit of madness, it appeared he who had once guarded the mount of God was doing just that.

A boom ripped the sky and the ground beneath me trembled; I feared the hill might give way, so I readied my wings. I could not discern what caused the explosion, but it continued on. No longer as extreme, but as a rolling thunder, it pounded up into the mount in which I still hid. I glanced around and behind trying to discern the origin of the explosion that shook the mounts and rocks around me, until I realized it was Lucifer. The High Lord spoke.

"*Brothers of the Hosts, long have we served, long have we toiled in the creation set before us, long have we trusted, praised, and adored the One who called us forth! For what seems as ages have we passed on in our time oblivious to the nature of our 'Father!' For as long as we have trusted, He has schemed. For as long as we have praised, he has plotted, and for every time we adored Him, He found the flaws within us that would excuse His vengeance, destroy His mistake, and erect His new perfection!"*

The Accuser continued, rolling charge after charge against the Father, yet the palace stood quiet, the gates remained closed. Nevertheless, Lucifer refused to slow his tirade. He raged against the Lord, and silence gripped the ranks as his hatred simmered in his words. Terror spread through me, not for the Father, or the Hosts, but for the violence I knew the Second prepared to unleash. I continued to stare and study our guardian cherub, wondering if our Lord would ever arise. Something kept Him from destroying His own, even in the face of open rebellion. I almost believed then that He was waiting for something. Dread sparked in my mind as an idea came upon me. What if the Father *feared* His own creation? What if He simply could not destroy the bearer of blasphemy standing within sight of His walls? My doubt grew while the wrath of the Second burned on.

"No longer will we bow in humble fear! No longer shall we kneel and remain blind to the plans of our demise!" He turned to the citadel as more words slid venomously from His tongue. *"Your time has come, 'Almighty God!' Now is the time of your children and their screams will stain your walls red while you sit weeping on your throne. Now is the time for your fall! Now is the hour for you, Creator, to tremble with us all and taste the fear of your making!"*

As the crash of his words echoed off the palace, Lucifer once more turned to address his army. The thundering rip of his words split the sky and echoed back unto me, deafening me to the distinct words he used, while reinforcing the anger and hatred within them. As I watched, the Legions swarmed forward as if a mass of liquid, flowing into emptiness. My breath caught; I stared unmoving. I froze. A son of God, crafted from nothing but chaotic power and I played the part of a coward. Soon after, the saddest sound heaven ever knew flowed through what remained of its dying purity, a cry of war.

The Host pulsed forward, faster, unchecked, resolute, and terrible. My fear shackled me. I exhaled, and became amongst the first to weep for what I saw. I cried for what was, for what I even then beheld, for those I would never know again, and for the coward I had become. I hid my face from the plains below while gazing off at the horizon. I sat with my back to the mount where moments ago I had been laying across its crest.

I no longer cared. I wished for the end, however it came. Then I heard the sound that changed my existence forever. The voice of my friend.

"Hold, *Captain!*" The sound of defiance, barely a breeze compared to the gale that blew before it, hardly reached my ears as I hastily climbed to the top once again, peering down, trying to locate the source of the voice.

"This shall not be the day of which you dreamed! From on high you shall be cast down! From the height of your pride you shall fall, and I shall be the witness for the Lord *Our* God!"

The pulse of my existence paused as I stared at the scene below. Due to my brief episode of pity and hopelessness, I had not seen from where the speaker had emerged, but now I beheld him. Alone, small, and seemingly insignificant, he stood against the Legions of Heaven, whom for a brief moment, abruptly stopped in utter disbelief of what stood before them.

There, on the steps of the palace, the Battle in Heaven was joined. On one side the Hosts were arrayed, led by the power and glory of the Second, and there, standing directly before the horrors of Lucifer himself, was Novation.

IV

The Deceiver's voice issued forth, no longer mixed with the roar of a multitude, but lavished in the eloquence of his words. "Novation, little one, you stand betrayed. Do not force us to destroy you, pawn. I will not hesitate to protect those offering their lives in the hopes of liberty and truth."

"I will not force you to destroy me, *Second,* but I will pressure you to defend yourself, for you will not assail these steps." My small friend's situation seemed a hopeless pursuit for a lost cause, a forgotten cause. An endless number of eyes gazed at him as his still, small voice breathed defiance into the face of his former lord. "You may turn back, or be cast down forever."

"You dare threaten *me,* Lesser. You are no more than a messenger, a joke of an object by which God can implement his compassion and pity! I wish none of the deceived to be thrown from their places, but I will not listen to your petty objections. As you see, the gates remain closed. Your *Father* fears for His existence, for He sees me approaching to cast Him down!"

As the Second's last word blew through the sky, darkness descended, as something changed deep within him. The colorless robes that knew all colors coalesced and solidified, rippling and conforming to his massive frame. Soon, his once soft and glorious robes turned into hardened, tempered plates of indestructible Essence. The flames in his eyes shot out above and below as his six wings carried him, barely above the ground. His armor grew tighter, constricting the core of our once glorious captain, until his perfect frame became descriptively outlined by his new Shaping. His chest, arms, torso, and legs were encased in glowing, pulsing material. His hair grew even brighter as power coursed through him, forming a ring of unbearable light that perched atop his head like a crown.

The very fabric of heaven seemed to seep into his body. He stretched out his arms as he gathered unto them the Essence he sought to wield. His hands crashed together, and the small space between his hands grew bright as it crackled and fizzed with blue light. His full, bright eyes were closed until now, but just as he drew his arms apart they flew open. The flames, once orange and fiery, now radiated scorching white energy as they danced upon his face. The hands, that had moments ago been pressed together, now held themselves out wide to either side revealing a monstrous, two-handed instrument that glowed and pulsed with the power that flowed through its maker.

Our Guardian Cherub grabbed one end and slowly glided it through the air. At one moment it radiated with a sickly green aura, and the next instant, ridged, blue lights arced along its length. The tool seemed to be clear, and within it I could make out deep, dark liquids flowing and mixing within the blade. One of the two appeared to be the color of what I learned later as resembling the blood of Man, while the other, a dark, fearsome violet, flowed over-whelmingly throughout the inside of what our Second had molded for his use. Thus, the first weapon of heaven was forged. I later grew to understand it when I eventually grasped its true name: *Sword.*

My disbelief captivated me as madness reigned below. I held my side view of the events taking place while watching Novation disappear from my sight by walking towards Satan, and behind a pillar. I gazed at the column that blocked him from my vision, but could not locate him. Just as I turned back to watch the Sec-ond in his state of unrestrained power and transformation, the battle began. Until then, Lucifer's head had slowly arced higher and higher, gazing farther and deeper into the heavens above, yet just as he began to lower his face and glare at his opponent a blast ripped the battlefield as the proud Captain's head snapped back, spinning him around as he fell to his knees, catching himself with wings and fists.

My gaze flashed back to the palace gates, and there stood my friend. He now approached from behind the column, pacing steadily toward the leader of the hosts. His hair, once short and bright, now flared with holy energy as it waved back and forth across the small of his back. His compassionate green eyes blazed dangerously with righteous rage. His hands were clinched at his side as he stepped towards his humbled enemy. A dim remnant of Essence resided in his fists, waiting for their release yet again. His robes remained, but they now emanated a light that no longer shown as green, but more of a shifting collage of colors that one now sees in the ocean, never knowing where one color ends and the other begins.

In one moment the Second of Heaven was falling, but he now stood risen again in unrivaled wrath.

"*Fool!* You stand before the Traitor's house and dare to give him your service. You are no better than He, self-proclaimed god though He be. You have damned yourself by your actions here today," hissed the Accuser as spittle fell from his lips. "Where there was once mercy for you, there is no longer."

"You are wrong, Fading Star. Even now, you die where you stand. Your spirit shall fade into the ages to come, and you will know the torment of your own eternity. Even now you dim before me. As the Morning Star you were upheld, but even there your pride found you. Just as the stars shall fall from their appointed places, so shall you streak from the sky! Satan I name you, and in that name, Accuser, shall you be thrown down!" My little friend never stopped walking towards the blasphemer of his Father, of our Father.

"You have chosen to fight. So shall it be." Satan's voice changed. It no longer raged incoherently at the smaller brother standing before him, yet it still brooded in hatred and spite for his challenger.

"Then come, Satan! At me! Here I stand, and here I shall fall! May my Father see me and sustain me. By His strength I shall see you plummet; by my hand or by the one who even now is watching!"

A roar riveted the boundaries of heaven, shaking the hills and plains therein as it billowed from the Chief of Princes. He rushed at my brave, little friend. Satan's sword rose and crashed right where I last saw my brother. A thunderclap lanced through the battlefield as the Hosts beheld the inconceivable. The weapon hung poised over Novation, who had somehow blocked the sword with an unseen power. As Satan stood frozen over his underestimated adversary, Novation reached up with his left hand, latching onto the Captain's forearm. A hiss whispered up to me as my friend melted a portion of the Second's impenetrable armor.

They stared at each for the briefest of seconds before Satan flung his arm back while wheeling around again with his sword. This time, as his blade struck Novation's "shield," Satan withdrew his right hand from the hilt and placed his hand, open palmed, a short distance from Novation's face. An instant later, a searing, bright light incinerated the spot where my brother had been standing. The beam of Essence fully enveloped my friend.

I could not breathe. My vision blurred. As resolute as he was, Novation could not have survived. I waited for the debris and dust to settle, and then I saw my friend. He trembled on his feet as his body quivered where he stood. He swayed back and forth, his eyes appeared dimmed, and I watched with horror as they slowly faded into darkness, his limp body falling forward into the dust that darted away from Heaven's second sin, murder.

"*Nooooo!*"

My scream rocketed over the hosts as I forgot myself and my place. I no longer cared for my safety. I no longer wondered whether the rumors were true. If that fallen spawn could destroy one as pure as my old friend, so also could he deceive the hosts for his will.

My brothers all turned to where I now hovered, silhouetted against the sky. My shimmering wings arced behind me, pulsing and growing as my rage enshrouded me. I felt my eyes grow hot and fierce as my wrath ignited an aura of blinding light that bound me within its brilliance.

I streaked toward my motionless friend. I did not even glance to the one who had stricken him. I kneeled down, slowly rolling him over. His hair had once again grown short and dim, and his robes were covered in a warm, dull colored liquid. When I saw that his eyes were open I grew hopeful, but then I noticed how dark they had become. They did not notice me, nor did they any longer flutter in life, but smoldered and sat unmoving in death, the first among creation. My friend was gone.

Alone. All alone, I sat surrounded by brothers who betrayed me, who betrayed Novation. Their leader did murder before me. Warm, shimmering liquid fell from my eyes in perfect, small drops. I caught one in my hand, and realized they were pieces of my Essence. Filled with light, their warmth caressed my face as they fell for my friend. They fell not for sorrow's sake, but for wrath's.

I let the drop slide from my hand as I rose and faced my *Captain*. "*You...,*" I began as menace leaked from my voice, but I could not finish. My own power silenced me.

"You what? Kaos, is it? What do you weep for? The passing of a friend or the ignorance he showed till the end? Do not make the same mistake, or you too will lie beside him."

"You have *destroyed*, Usurper. For that, you must be judged."

"By who? You?" Satan scoffed. "You have not even found your purpose. You are nothing more than a fluttering mistake to remind our God of why we must be removed. You are an embarrassment! Did you enjoy witnessing the death of your friend from that hill? Did you see him fall before me? Not only are you without purpose, Kaos, your cowardice seems to know no bounds."

My eyes closed and brimmed over with the same white drops that mimicked the tears from before. I failed my friend. I watched him fall. Now, I had but two choices. Doubt filled me for a brief moment, until then I remembered the sweet of voice of a brother I would never hear again. *Where will you stand, Kaos? Where will you stand?* I would never fail my friend again.

My arms arched and curled at my side as I stooped over bended knees. Soon, my robes also grew constricted and tight. Hardened with righteousness and sorrow, my Essence took the shape of glowing, blue armor. My hair grew long and bright as it fell over my eyes and face. I was briefly blinded as light shot from my eyes. I felt my face grow warm and eventually hot to the touch. I could soon tell my face glowed as I caught glimpses of sizzling energy sliding up and down along my peripheral vision. Not only my robe, but my own skin crystallized before my eyes, molding, melting, cooling, and tempering as it rolled over itself, each fold finding its allotted space. My arms slowly relaxed as my hands unclenched; myriads of color danced upon the ground as my own form became a living prism. The liquid light that poured from my eyes hissed as its vaporous state steamed from my face.

As I neared the climax of my purification, a tearing, ripping pain slashed at my back. Impossible as it should have been for an enemy to pierce my new form, I still feared for my lack of control; I was unable to stop my Essence. The pain grew in intensity, maturing into torturous agony as I stood, back arched, arms thrown wide, a scream hiding in the back of my throat. Two great explosions of power suddenly tore through my crystallized shell and burnished armor as two great wings, each as wide as my own height twice over, shrieked from my back and flung themselves apart, as if gasping for a restricted breath.

My mouth clamped shut as my head lowered, eyes closed in thought. My coupled pairs of wings took positions around me. The two, being newly formed, continued their flexed reach towards the sky as they grew wider and brighter. My previous wings enshrouded my diamond-coated arms as they glided gracefully towards the grass of heaven.

My wrath subsided, but my grief reigned in any possibility of pride at my new form. Novation, or that which had once been my friend, lay encrusted in the dirt that caught his fall. I turned with the touch of new found grace, and knelt at the side of my little hero.

His name fell from my lips as a timid whisper, but he did not hear me. My Essence crackled and danced round my jeweled arm, yet it shook in weakness as I reached towards the first friend I had ever failed.

"Novation?" I breathed his name a second time, but his head only rolled limply with the merest touch of my hand. Then my spirit broke, and my Essence-filled light leapt in miniature streaks that encircled the corpse of my brother, repeatedly striking the

ground in rage and sorrow. My long hair lightened the underside of my face as it fell with my head towards my chest. My pride shattered and fled from me as I slid my arms beneath the limp body before me, cradling it to my trembling chest. Its head hung dead from my arms, its arms and legs, dimmed and lightless, dragged through the dust as I slowly rose. I knew not what needed to be done.

Death was not a word we knew, yet there it lay, incarnate in my arms as my own tears fell upon its cold, lightless face. Where do you place the vilest of curses? How do you hide your deepest shame?

Bearing my new found burden, I turned to stare into the eyes of my first enemy.

V

"And I expelled you, O guardian cherub…"

-Ezekiel 28:16-

My friend's corpse hung from my grasp as I stood unmoving before the evil that took him from me. Satan was no lord, and any station once given him would be stripped away, by my hand or the by the One who made me. I stared into the tainted chaos that ripened within the depths of Satan's eyes, while he saw the madness that I knew now ripened within my own.

My former Captain gazed curiously back at me. I no longer feared him. The fear of my own destruction became nothing more than a hollow thought in the back of my mind. This assurance sprang not from pride, but from ignorance. Even as his gaze betrayed his concern, he deceived me. Even as I turned my back again to him and strode towards the Palace steps, he enacted his plan. I knew not his power.

"You turn your back on your own destruction, Kaos."

His words sounded empty to me. What else could he do? He had taken from me the most precious of the Father's gifts, Life. Now torn from those I had once loved, only a small thread of sorrow and vengeance kept me tied to this creation. I almost wished

I too could fall into the sleep of annihilation, of the Nothing from which I came.

My legs ached from power and grief as they strode towards the gate of the Throne. The mouth of my dead friend hung open as small rivulets of light trickled down his face. His eyelids poised half open, but the beauty and light of his eyes had fled, leaving two deep, dark pits of lightless horror.

There came movement behind me. I felt them before I saw them. I held our dead brother, and still they came at me. I acted as if they were not there. I climbed the steps towards the door of my Father's Throne. They closed, sneaking, as if they thought me ignorant of their cowardice. I laid my friend at my feet; his limp weight slid from my arms and came to rest at the very doors for which he died. I closed my eyes and breathed in my last moment of peace, before I chose the path that destroyed it.

The first came at my left, but my glimmering hand streaked toward his neck, snapping it as my eyes clinched shut and one last tear fell. I turned to my aggressor, forcing myself to watch as his life seeped from his eyes as they had left Novation's. A moment's hesitation gripped me, accusing me as the murderer I was damned to become, but it soon fled when I again saw the shell of my brother lying at my feet. There was no hate, only wrath, at what had to be done and for those who had forced Heaven's Mandate upon me.

I turned in time to see at least ten more of my former brothers circling me, eyeing me, hating me. None were as anxious as the first, however. I knew them once, yet as they came at me, I found I could no longer recognize them. Their eyes seemed different, abnormal, and alien, proving that I was now truly alone. Alone, as Novation had been before he fell, but I would not fall. I could not fall. Not yet.

"Your own brothers call for your downfall, traitor!"

"You are the traitor, Satan! Your words have slid from me as they slid from the walls of the citadel you seek to raze. Your lies are no more, your schemes are no more, and soon, you will fade from this place as my friend has faded from me!" Even as I challenged the Second, my eyes danced amongst the deceived who came at me. They completely encircled me, and as I watched, began shaping armor and weapons of their own. Some fashioned thick lengths of solid light with a barbed hook upon either end. Others carved out double-bladed spears, single and two-handed swords, maces, flails, and axes, none of which we knew when they were first formed. Behind the heads of his pawns, I saw Satan grin.

"*Destroy him,* before he snatches away the salvation of our kind."

The Legions stood behind the usurper. Endless ranks of hate and rebellion faded off to my right and left. I could only see several ranks behind Satan as I gathered myself for the imminent onslaught. He held the might of the Hosts in his grip, along with weapons formed from his once untainted Essence, and I stood alone against them all. Yet I had watched my friend burn with my own eyes, I knew the lies of my former prince, and I shook with agony as I felt my Father's own sorrow and wrath fill me. I became a vessel of retribution for an unseen God as I received the deepest of my pained desires, vengeance.

They rushed at once; three fell headless as my arm returned to my side following an outpouring of my own Essence. My legs coiled as I crouched; my arms flexed and curled at my sides as my clinched fists pulsed and shook. My right wing sent two more staggering off to my side as I spun into the air. White brilliance flashed from my right arm, and then dimmed as another of my former brothers vaporized in front of me.

I heard their screams; I saw their Essence leak and flow from their wounds, but my eyes no longer knew compassion and my spirit felt calloused since Novation fell. I did not stop, could not stop, and those who assailed me continued to scream.

The first rank now marched on me. A beam of light knocked back my shoulder, but my left arm swung quickly in front, palm open to the source of my pain before I watched as my own light lacerated one of the Second's foremost troops. For a while, I lost all recollection of what followed. The screams faded from my ears as the carnage flowed over my eyes and stuck to my armor. Still they sought to assail me as Satan continued to grin. My hardened skin glimmered and flashed as my arms launched Essence into those nearest me.

The lifeless stacked below me as I hovered over the steps to the Throne. Novation's body remained untouched, and I kept it so. I still do not know whether Satan tired of the massacre or grew weary of waiting, but he called back his troops. I heaved and gasped as lightning danced around my burnished form. Several dozen of my former brothers lay broken around me, while many more I knew were torn from the very fabric of existence. Slowly, my breathing calmed and my seething eyes grew focused as I lowered myself to the ground.

Satan grinned down at me, as if impressed with my efforts. He could have easily overwhelmed me if he only let the hosts march forward. In my new state I would have destroyed many of them, but would have ultimately fallen. He glanced sideways at the ranks reforming around him, before casting his gaze again upon me. The grin turned maniacal as his crazed eyes burned their images deep into my memories. Then the Second spoke.

"Impressive, Lesser. You should have fallen many times over by now, yet you continue to sow your hatred. I would be mindful, Kaos, of what you intend to reap."

"Quit your deceptions, Satan. Here I stand, and you have yet to throw me down. Your pride has swollen your mind along with your false power. You will reap your own reward soon enough."

"Our kind were never meant to be alone, Kaos. Yet you stand as such against all those who once loved you, against those who called you, 'brother.' How long do you think it will last, fool? Every second you stand before me is another fragment in time that proves to me our Father is a coward indeed. He is not what He seems, Kaos. You know this. How could such a God allow His child to perish? *Look!* There is your proof, son of God!" His shimmering finger trembled in rage as it pointed directly behind me, where Novation lay.

I turned my head and gazed along the ranks. Without number or equal, they waited. What hope did I have? Could I be wrong? No. I was not wrong, but did that mean I would not lose everything in this sacrifice? I was guaranteed nothing, except every moment that I passed alive. All those I once held dear glared back at me. All along the ranks I saw their eyes flaring, like so many ravenous predators in the dark. That was when I knew them for what they were. I seemed an insignificant light compared to what loomed ahead, but even so I found a peace amidst that chaos, a peace which I could never describe.

"You murdered, Novation, Deceiver. Never forget that. As far as your insignificant rebellion, it will last as long as the Father wills it to be, and so shall your remaining time in His presence. You were never in control, Satan, and any power once given you even now seeps from your grasp. Drive me from *your* presence if you can, Second, or do you fear a true servant of One who laughs at your childish boasts?"

"*Silence!* You dare to proclaim authority over me! I stood at the Word's side when He sculpted your filth from chaos! I guarded the very mount upon which the Father stood when he whispered the stars into the sky! I have seen the fire of His Throne, the Wheels that carry it, and it will be mine!" Thunder and madness carried Satan's words to me as my ears squealed and rang with each cry, but he would not silence me.

"I have been held in the arms of the Creator! I knew a love you have forgotten! I laughed on the banks of the Rivers to Come, and lounged in peace by the Trees of Life! I remember when the Stars used to praise God instead of curse Him! I knew fear and darkness, until I found the face of Him who called me from it! You have forgotten your place, Accuser, and just as you have forgotten, so shall Heaven forget you!"

"Enough! I know the plans of the 'Father,' and if you wish to be cursed by His deception I will not stop you. Yet do *not* hinder me from preserving those amongst us who have foreseen the lies to come. We have eyes to see, and so we have seen. You are a blind mistake, Kaos. When I reign over everything you see before you, I will call up no mercy for those who did not stand at my side."

The challenges faded into silence as I stared at the prince I once glorified and followed. I stood motionless as bolts of Essence arced through and over my crystallized skin before rushing into the ground. Satan's eyes flared blood red for the merest hint of an instant before they gleamed gold again, before he proclaimed my verdict.

"*So be it.*"

It sounded as if the Legions had roared in unison, but I knew the voice to be Satan's. His head flung back as the foundation of Heaven shook beneath us all. Before me, Satan shook and threw himself into the throes of his power. The six wings stretched and flexed behind and around him as his armor grew brighter, flashing thunderbolts into the sky. Cackling light leapt and jumped from his body to the ground. My right foot slid back and anchored itself as I slowly crouched. Cupping my hands together I cradled my last hope within my hands. Satan's scream faded and calmed even as his frame bulked and swelled. His head lowered, and I found myself looking into the eyes of hate incarnate.

Then he was upon me.

VI

In a flash my hands smacked apart with a hiss, forming my own weapon. It burned bright unto my eyes as I drew it from my own Essence. Broad and strong it balanced in my hand as the purest of white bolts danced along its edge. Energy cackled and hummed down its length as I leveled it before my eye. My first sword poised in my grip.

We clashed around the foundation of my Father's palace. I never understood why he did not simply send forth his Legions. If our God had really lost his authority they could have assaulted the throne room while I fought their lord. The ranks stood unmoving, however, following us along with their gazes as their eyes matched the movement of our swords.

The thunderous crashing of our blades numbed my ears as my hilt shuddered in my hands. Long did we rage in the sky above Heaven, applying untested skills to unknown tools. We continued to test, pry, and vie for the weakness of the other, but no such flaw was found. He was the Second, and I was Kaos, wrought in vengeance. In my eyes there burned no weakness.

"I have wearied myself with your contentions, Kaos. It is time for you to rest alongside your brother." We had stopped only for a moment before this prince taunted my efforts. He spoke as such to no avail, however, for I stood foolish in my power. I thought I could win.

"Why do you tarry, Satan? Do you fear the reckoning made ready for you, or do you draw strength from your words and lies?" My challenge ended; I made ready for his rebuttal.

"I have but toyed with you, child. By the end of your next breath, I will cast you down; you will become nothing more than another instrument by which I hold sway over the Hosts."

"Then *at me,* Lucifer, Morning Star! Cast me down if you ca..." The last word barely escaped over my shimmering lips before my glorified state slammed into the ground, coupled with an explosion of sound and color.

"*Fool! I am at thee! I am upon you! I am the Prince, the Dawn and the Morn! It is I you called and a God who answered! Who are you, fallen seraph? Rise at me, Lesser, and claim back your pride!*"

I could neither move nor breathe. Light-filled liquid spat from my mouth as I leaned on quivering arms and legs. My vision clouded while my senses reeled. Where had he hit me? I began to rise, but he grabbed me around the neck, holding me aloft. My two great wings draped the ground as he raised me with the full extension of his arm.

"Did you really think you could oppose me, Kaos? And you, the one who kills his own brothers to get to me, to what did it all avail? What a waste. So, who commits the greater evil, *Lesser?* One who kills for need, or one who murders in vengeance?"

In those fleeting seconds all my hopes were forgotten. To fight and die would be a greater call for honor than to flee and live, and as such I stood. Whether I stood for Truth or lies I did not yet know; I thought I would never know. All that mattered is that I resisted.

"I was never to be… your judge, *traitor.* He is yet to co… come." Essence and slurred words gurgled from my gasping throat. One of my legs twitched as the prismatic light it held shivered along the ground. The hand gripping my enemy, almost set to burn his arm and wrist, grew dull and dim. My smaller wings, once risen above, now drooped below, clutching at the dust.

"That's it, Kaos. *Sleep.* To sleep with you; forget the damnation nigh upon you. To sleep." My once bright eyes flared feverishly for a fleeting instant before they dimmed and faded into darkness. As the reality of death deluged my mind, questions arose before they immediately vanished. How could he have played me for a fool for so long? How could anyone oppose his power? I feared the answers to my doubts. Even as I pondered over what may come, I grew forgetful, my vision faded, and my sword fell from my dimming hand. As it clanged upon the stones below, my fading senses caught another sound. A voice, one I had forgotten.

"Put the child down, Prince. Your fight is with *me* now."

The Second, turning, dropped me to the ground, and glared at the one who spoke. I managed to roll over and catch my breath in time to witness doubt take birth in Satan's eyes. The challenger stood unadorned, clothed only in the purest of white linens. His snow white hair curled below his ears, and his eyes betrayed only the slightest hint of power while they glowed fiercely under his lashes. He stood a short distance from the doors of the Throne, as if he had just emerged, although no one seemed to have noticed them open. His eyes narrowed as he spoke to the taint before him.

"It is time, brother. You drive our Father into mourning. I have beheld great sorrow, and as such, I have come to silence the one who crafts it. I am the Message. Who is like God?! Are you, Lucifer? We were both there, Guardian Cherub. We witnessed Creation, yet you betray us all. Why? Do you not know? Have you not eyes, brother? Or, has your pride cursed your eyes along with your soul?"

"Raca! Fool of a Captain, do you think you will be spared when he disposes of the rest of his mistakes? Look at my Host. They have seen, and it will take more than you to blind them again, Miyka'el."

Miyka'el, Third to God Himself, stood glaring at the power and glory that was Satan. My mind reeled. I assumed that the absence of the remaining Chief Princes meant Satan had merely subjugated or disposed of them. Yet here stood the last, claiming to have been in the presence of God when the rebellion began. If that was true, where were the rest? And where was our Father?

"I am not alone, brother. Have you grown so blind? There is still hope for mercy, Morning Star. The destruction you have issued and warranted can be swept clean if you but turn aside now. You have no other ch…"

"Silence! Miyka'el, you among all the Archangels must know that this is *our* chance. There will be no other. Have you not seen it? You talk of my blindness, but you yourself can neither see nor hear the warnings before you. Why do you think He plots on Creating this 'Man?' Why do you think He reaches outside our Utopia to Shape again? We will and are being replaced even now! No, I will not turn aside nor bow to the false deity who betrays us even now." Satan grew still as his words for Miyka'el slithered into my thoughts, doubts being born all over again.

Miyka'el stood unmoving, unblinking. He remained as still and quiet as stone. "Do you wish to tell Him so, my Prince?" The term of respect shocked me, but I grew to learn that this was the last plead on Satan's behalf.

"I will, and you may be my witness, along with the armies of Sardis arrayed before you. You all will see the quivering 'god' whose reign ends now!" He spat the last word as he turned from his troops to face the Third once again.

Then Miyka'el turned his eyes aside, hiding them along with the light that filled them, beneath lids concealing his sorrow. For seconds mimicking eternity the entryway to the Throne fell silent and still. Then again did his eyes rise, but they were not the same. The glowing eyes once hinting at the prince's true power now flared dangerously in wrathful imminence.

"Then you shall do so through me and through the forces arrayed against you. My fallen brother, this above all else I swear. You shall never again enter into His house unguarded and without escort. You have been branded, and I have been given the charge to cast you from His presence." There was a brief pause as our Captain's oath passed over us all. "You have broken our Father's heart, brother... my Father's heart. He is no longer able to lay His eyes upon you."

I slowly rose during the discourse, still kneeling beside my faded sword, clinched in my hand. "Kaos." I failed to even notice the prince looking at me. "Your lack of action forced a weaker brother to lay down what you were not willing to lose. You, however, did cast aside the cowardice that held you down when Novation fell. You have been spared their fate, and they have chosen theirs. Come to me."

My weak legs gathered strength as I walked to the foot of the stairs. The Second's eyes bored into my crystallized frame as I walked before him. How could he have crippled me so quickly? I was as nothing to him, a pest that he swept from his shoulder. I lost my friend, my pride, and my future all at once. I possessed nothing else to offer my God, nothing else to sacrifice. Satan had taken it all from me.

"Of what force do you speak, Miyka'el?" Satan questioned as his eyes turned again to the Third. "There are none to oppose me but you and the Lesser."

"Soon, Satan. Very soon."

"And what is to keep me from killing you now and claiming that which is mine? I only toyed with that mistake beside you, but you I shall cast down in rage. I shall not be turned aside, not even by you, Miyka'el."

"You may assail me if you wish, Second, but your wisdom denies you the luxury of doing so. I will never be bested by the likes of you, Usurper. I will gladly silence your proud tongue before the remainder of Heaven is cursed to bear witness to your Fall, Shai'tan." The last word was spit, as a curse.

"You speak riddles, Third. There will be no Fall, only an Ascension, and you will bear witness to that; I promise you."

My body righted itself, my vision settled, and my mind began to focus once more. Even with Miyka'el at my side, I doubted what two could do against the army of Sardis. One lay stricken behind us, I seethed, humbled in my brokenness, and a friend I thought destroyed now stood humbly adorned in the face of the Legions. As I continued to think, Satan turned to address his followers.

"You have seen the proof! The Lord God 'Almighty' has brought us two Lessers and a proud fool to save Himself! The very God who Shaped us now cowers from us in hiding! His troops have abandoned Him, you have abandoned Him, I have abandoned Him, and now Heaven will abandon Him. This sweet day will pass forever into a Timeless memory that will be recalled as the day Truth drove out the deceit of our Maker!"

Satan continued screaming unto his Legions as Miyka'el gestured to me. "Kaos, we haven't much time. Before you stand roughly a third of heaven, but Lucifer is no fool. He gathered those with ability to fight, and shape, and think. His followers seem bred for war. Although the remainder of the hosts outnumbers this force before us, they would be torn to pieces. There are no fighters, few shapers, and none of them could enact stratagems given them. All that remains, barring a few, is a host of Lesser brothers bearing unwavering faith in the Father."

"So, what is there for us to do? If the Father knows we cannot win, why does He stay silent and bide His time? Novation is dead, Miyka'el, and I, even I, have done murder. There is nothing more for me to give."

"His lies have already blinded you. Your heart, son of God. Give to Him your heart. With that, this Flood can be turned aside. As for myself, I have been given charge to fight, Kaos, but I will not stand alone. Help is coming; the hand of the Father is always before and behind. They will be here soon."

"Help? Who can help us against that?" I gestured hopelessly to the legions before us. For a brief instant, it seemed Miyka'el also doubted.

"I know it seems hopeless, but I would rather be destroyed and wrenched back into the void from which I came, than made to serve that bastard son of God."

Miyka'el fell silent as Satan's roaring further inspired the once faithful soldiers of God; then he spoke to me again. "I have lived enough I think, Kaos. Before, I knew nothing, and I saw nothing. I loved nothing. But now I have walked, soared, sang, laughed, and loved. Now, thanks to the Second I have feared, doubted, and wept. I have seen what is to see, and if what comes after demands the absence of the One who gave it all, then I will gladly perish."

"Cannot God stop this? Why? Why does it go on? Is He not able to silence these lies? If He is, why does he not come to us?"

The Third exhaled a long, sad breath before turning his eyes to me. "My faith would say that He is able to do all things. It would also say that He could end this suffering at any time. As that faith so guides my words, so too must it guide my actions. Can God stop this madness? Perhaps so. Perhaps not, Kaos. Perhaps that is why we stand alone."

No. It could not be true. If we were God's only hope then what purpose was God? Why serve a defenseless entity? My thoughts combated themselves as I wrestled with what they implied. If we really were God's last chance, then why did Miyka'el offer his life? I looked off to my right to that still form which had once been my dear friend. Why did my brother die? Why did the weak suffer for the cowardice of the strong?

"…and for their blindness they shall suffer, but you shall live forever, safe from the world that is even now being molded for your destruction!" Satan turned from His Legions to face us once again.

"Your time is up, children. I suggest you step aside. My Time has come."

"He has given us knees of iron, Deceiver; we cannot bow to the likes of you."

"Ignorant, proud fools! If your knees refuse to bend for me then I shall shatter them so that you may lie at my feet!"

Miyka'el briefly turned his face to meet mine. "It is time, friend. Our help comes soon. Stand strong. Have faith, I will be there to guard you."

Doubts burdened my heart, and all my pain clouded my eyes once again. Why fight? Why go on? Our own God was hiding in His Palace. Why should I die for Him? Then I realized my greatest blessing. I could choose. I could fight for hope, or life, or love. I could fight for God, or Man, or Novation. Or I could do what I chose to do that dark, evil day. I fought to die.

With no words we rose and descended the steps before us. Breaths hissed through clenched teeth all throughout those dark ranks when they saw our eyes burning brighter with each slow, steady step. Twin fires, coupled in the same cause, burned bright and fierce in the depths of our eyes. They neither dimmed nor grew faint.

"Finally," hissed their fallen captain, "a true adversary by which to prove the weakness of God." All eyes followed Satan's lithe movements as he strode towards us, bearing down on Miyka'el. With a broad sweep, the first sword in heaven rose and fell upon my true captain, before Miyka'el caught the sharpened blade with his outstretched hand.

"Do not tease me, Lucifer. If you do not care to fight me with your true power, then I will gladly break you here before the mount of God." Miyka'el shoved the blade away. I stood motionless, barely thinking as time slowed to a crawl. I glanced towards Satan just in time to see his eyes begin to burn.

"*So be it, Third.* You shall see me for who I AM." Satan took a few slow steps away from the one who had turned him aside. What occurred soon after became the greatest perversion ever birthed upon the creation of God. Perfection ruined itself as beauty prostituted itself with evil. Thus, Beelzebub was born.

The Second's eyes clenched shut as he transformed before us. His six, perfect wings coalesced into two, gigantic expanses of leathery skin. Where once there had been light, only darkness now reigned. Veins and muscles rippled and curled throughout them as jagged talons peeked out along their tops. Even his skin turned dark, as if his very existence sucked light from the air. It remained hardened, except strange symbols formed along his breast and shoulders, red swirling images betraying the truth behind what Satan became that day. His arms stretched and pulsed under his dark armor as he doubled over. His back swelled and heaved. His hulking mass soon dwarfed both Miyka'el and me. His light-filled hair grew long and dark as its mange grew over his closed eyes.

"I am the Master of this House, Miyka'el. I suggest you submit."

My blazing eyes froze in fear and awe. Satan continued to change, continued to become that to which he had given birth, Sin. His dry, taut wings pulsed and stretched as his legs bulged and convulsed, forming two, gigantic black hooves stomping along the once holy ground. Hair grew and thickened, covering his entire body in a wooly mass that shrouded whatever glory he had once housed within himself. He traded his beauty for power, and I began to despair.

"Kaos, run. Hold back until the Chosen come. They will be here. Soon—I pray soon." His last words seemed spoken to no one.

My Captain's words snapped my mind back into the moment as I turned my eyes from a perversion to a prince. "Miyka'el, you cannot hold against him, against that! He becomes some unnamed evil. This is a perversion we were never meant to know. We must fly!"

Miyka'el's countenance fell as his eyes vacantly closed. "I have no choice. My Father has commanded me." His eyes rose and seared into my own. "Now go! Before *he* is complete, for then we shall both be made forfeit."

I looked from Satan, writhing as he was, back at my prince, then up into the sky of Heaven. "Is this the end of things, my Prince?"

He lowered his head in a moment of thought. Before he answered, his gaze followed my own into the stars. "All things end, little brother. But there are always new beginnings, when all the vaporous veils of this life will fade, pulling us back from the pains of this world, only to usher in the joy of a new one. We will rest on those new shores, Kaos. Perhaps today, or much later, when the ages run dark and gray, leaving angels to themselves to weep and remember such wars as these."

I soberly nodded before I reluctantly flew away.

VII

"*Resist the devil, and he will flee from you.*"

-James 4:7-

My blazing wings swept me backward, higher and farther away from coming onslaught. I continued on until I reached a ledge. There I crouched like a gargoyle upon the side of my Father's Palace. My large wings balanced me while their smaller counterparts swept the roof where I sat. My hands glowed and pulsed as I waited, gripping the ledge while my flaring eyes followed the scene below.

Miyka'el remained unmoving as his former prince shook and writhed with his new found power. Satan's head shot back as his perfect teeth elongated into fangs, jagged and crooked, twisted terribly from what they were originally intended to be. A roar leapt from his throat as his eyes bulged and widened. The Prince of Heaven gambled with the Sin of his heart in a battle of control; he was losing. His very heart grew weak against the perversion he birthed. It was an act of incarnation, sin becoming flesh.

The bestial ravings flying from the throat of the Second ripped into the hearts of all who heard them. The Hosts aligned against the Father backed away from their leader. This was madness, and madness knew no ally.

Miyka'el did not move or raise his eyes to meet his enemy, the being that once was Satan. The howls of Beelzebub waned and grew quiet as the transformation drew to a close. All that was perfect was forfeit, made as a sacrifice for the high priest of Sin reaping his damned reward.

Beelzebub's bulging, maniacal eyes glared at the Third who remained unmoving. Eyelids made of thick, dark canvas slid and scratched over the orbs that proved the insanity of the Second. Why didn't Miyka'el move? The silence was maddening, and I almost left my post, if not to do anything but fill that empty time with sound. And then the perversion spoke.

"Miiiyyykaaa'eeelll... Miiiyyykaaa'eeelll... Do you see me, Third? Open your eyes, former brother, and behold your new *God.*" His voice sent my mind reeling. I grabbed at my chest as a wave of malice swept over me. Light blurred itself around my eyes as all evil branded my mind and soul. Having known no dark thing before that day, I could not adjust to seeing the one who created what God had not, Sin. If it hindered Miyka'el he gave no sign. Still and resolute, he stared silently into the ground at his feet before he breathed judgment into the face of the Fallen.

"I no longer know you, brother. What once was has been struck down. Your power has made you powerless. You are no longer master, but a slave to the pride that has deceived you thus far. You boast in things you no longer know, for what you boasted was resemblance to the One you now oppose. Now you are like no one, and nothing will ever resemble you again. Even if you find your power, you have ordained yourself to remain alone for eternity, and in that loneliness shall your madness be fed. Now flee this place, or I shall drive you from it."

Beelzebub did not move a muscle, but his breathing slowly deepened and grew stronger. Each pant and breath brought snot and spittle to the Beast's mouth. Dripping resemblances of liquid Essence, now crimson or violet, splattered and hissed on the ground.

His eyes rolled back, revealing red, blue, and black veins lining his eyes, each filled with a dark fluid broiling in his hatred, replacing every trace of his fleeting purity. His long arms flexed and contorted as his talons clawed and tore at the earth. Then Sin roared.

The explosion from his throat flew through heaven. Every angel within my sight bent over, clutching at his ears. I noticed them briefly as my hands pawed at my own. The scream pierced my thoughts as everyone cowered under its power, except for Miyka'el. He seemed not even to breathe. His face still pointed towards the ground as his eyes remained closed. The roar came to an end, Heaven ceased its shaking; and then Miyka'el moved.

His face rose as his eyes opened, and an inferno flew from his eyes. The flames licked his curled hair and spread back over his face. Raw power imploded into his back, and monolithic wings shot out. Traced in Essence and pulsing in their power, six of them stretched and arched towards the sky, but their bearer remained on the ground. His simple robes did not coalesce as mine had, but were consumed in the fire of his flesh. In a twinkling where there had once been garments of service and worship, there now sat armor molded for war and destruction.

Miyka'el's face began to glow as light ricocheted from the burnished casing which housed his power. The armor rose to either side of his face, hiding his shoulders deep where no enemy could reach. Angelic symbols and names of the Orders curled and slid down his chest, beaming from the plate that made him seemingly invulnerable. Telanos, Istanos, Executus, Xalius, Nephitirim, Eternios, and more were all molded into his shimmering form. Some of which, if not most, now sat armed against the one who bore their name. I twitched my wings as I tried to catch a glimpse of the other names, before Miyka'el screamed.

The bellow came from the deepest reaches of his Essence, where most angels cannot reach or know. His arms stretched taut to either side, quaking in the power pouring over them. As Miyka'el's cry reached its climax, a boiling, writhing stream of scalding Essence gushed from the Third's mouth and onto the ground at his feet. Where the liquid fell, the ground melted away. All the while, swirling spheres of light and power enshrouded the Captain and his glorification. Confused as to what he planned I watched Miyka'el closely, before I saw the weapons.

To the left of where he stood a towering shaft shot from the ground topped with a point carved from diamonds. A hilt followed Miyka'el's spear that still dripped Essence as it rose from the ground. Fountains of light spewed from the earth as Miyka'el's sword continued to rise. Its blade was broad, double-edged, and adorned with the Word. Such markings could never be forged into a blade, only spoken. The Father had breathed over the very thing Miyka'el now drew from the ground.

Even as I watched, its colors danced and collided with each other. At one moment blue, then red, then white, then green, the blade continued to change. The light of the Third's weapons ricocheting off his armor constructed a prism of undeniable power that glowed and pulsed over the Legions surrounding him. My Prince grew calm while the flames in Miyka'el's eyes dimmed, leaving two piercing blue orbs, glaring at the perversion before him.

And Heaven was silent.

VIII

"You were filled with violence, and you sinned. So I drove you in disgrace from the mount of God..."

-Ezekiel 28:16-

There they stood, monoliths of tainted and untainted power, perfect opposites. Satan, hunched and gnarled, brooding and frothing in his own disgusting power, towered only a short distance from Miyka'el who stood frozen in Time. The light from the Prince cast a blue hue over the creature before him, but any light that ventured near the face of the Devil disappeared into those fathomless pits that perched within the Beast's head.

"You cannot win, Miyka'el. It is hopeless." Satan's words crawled from his mouth by way of the long, forked, and slithering tongue rolling around his lips.

"The promise of victory was never given to me; only to the One yet to come. I have only been commanded to fight, and any hope I have will never be founded on my own strength."

Satan's maw gaped open and stretched as his teeth gnashed together. Miyka'el hunched down as he raised his spear and sword from the earth. Both sat motionless for a second that seemed to span an eternity. Miyka'el's eyes flashed brilliant for an instant before the former prince fell upon heaven's champion.

The left claw streaked out; Miyka'el smashed away the attack with his sword as his spear rose in defense against what Satan shaped in his hand. It was the same blade as the first, yet no longer beautiful. It wreaked of evil; dark, crimson droplets dripped off the blade, splashing bloodily on the ground. Jagged and twisted, its edge fell on the spear, and even its burnished ore, molded in the heart of heaven, gave off sparks of gleaming brilliance as it creaked and groaned under the onslaught.

The two titans of heaven battled on as Miyka'el's eyes grew fierce with power and wrath. I could see the hatred in his eyes, even though his voice remained still and quiet—hatred not for the brother he once embraced, but for the creature that perverted him. For that did he battle and for that did the cry from his soul beg for a lost friend's destruction.

Satan snarled and snapped, slinging acidic Essence all over his former brother. His sizzling spit tore away at the flesh on Miyka'el's face. Even as his burnt skin smoldered and fell away, there came no cry, no look of pain, only a look of vengeance for that which consumed his brother. As the acid boiled and crawled down his face, tears from Miyka'el's eyes mixed within its searing descent, mingling with the liquid still scarring his perfect face.

They broke apart for the briefest moment, only to hurl themselves into the sky, before they joined again. Satan's leathery perversions flapped thunder in the air as Miyka'el's powerful wings screamed sorrow through the sky. Blades crashed and roared as the spear groaned but held true.

For hours they battled; neither faltered. One warred for hate and pride, the other for love and for love lost. I watched my Captain, I watched my former prince, and I saw the body of my friend crumpled near the steps below me. My sorrow broke, and as I wept the battle raged on. I could do nothing but behold this great sorrow as it played out before me.

Again they broke, hovering in the sky of heaven, staring unmoving at the other. The madness in Satan's eyes flashed as they rolled over themselves in indescribable disgust, while the passion in Miyka'el's burned fiercely over the tear stains of spent sorrow.

"Lucifer, Child of the Morning. Hear me, Brother! Your time has come! If you will not turn I will annihilate you and leave you ruined throughout all the ages!"

"*Lucifer!? HeheHeHaHaHAHA!* That name is no more, fool of fools! I have Lucifer now, and what he ever was is dead! There is only me. *Sin!* Know me now, for *I am* your enemy!" In that moment the vile insanity flung itself from the mouth of Beelzebub and blasphemy took shape. *I am.*

The promise barely slid from the creature's forked tongue before a roar overshadowed the depravity that dripped from the Beast's oozing maw. "Then I am yours! And I, *you* will know! My name is *Miyka'el!* Who is like God!? Here I stand, Fallen Star! You will crash deep into the surf of the world our Father prepares! Feast on my vengeance, for in my wrath I will drown you while the decrees of the Almighty God burn in your soul for eternity!"

The Chief Prince paused in his oath long enough to close his eyes, breathing a silent prayer before he issued his challenge and lament. "Goodbye, brother. You I will always love, and in that love I must destroy you. Farewell."

"Save your pity, *Prince!* I will feast on you yet. Steel yourself, and look me in the eye!"

Before they could again join, Miyka'el suddenly arched back and above Sin, pulled back his spear, and hurled it with unknown strength towards the earth. I failed to notice, but those who followed the perversion of Lucifer had risen from the ground and were stealthily stalking towards the Palace Gate, and myself. The

Spear of the Archangel careened into the earth, incinerating from existence a score of angels as they instantly vanished in smoke and ruin. The rest fell back momentarily as their brothers disappeared, but not before a chasm tore itself into the fabric of heaven, dragging even more into the chaos of nonexistence below. It tore apart the shelf alongside the foundation of the Palace. Nearby, the traitorous brothers paused in their retreat as they flashed hate-filled looks towards their dominant enemy.

The angels' temporary shock faded, however, and they soon gathered into a joint rage as they hurled themselves towards my Captain. The Legion rose up as one wave, one force, against our last remaining hope. I could no longer sit by and watch. I lost one friend; I would not lose my last.

With my own cry for battle I rose. My body hardened, my wings stretched and glowed, and I hurled myself into that which opposed my God—my Father. The surprise took them at first, for their attention was diverted, but their focus soon fell upon me.

"Here we stand, Kaos! Be strong, for He is *watching!*" My eyes gleamed brilliant as I heard his words. Light pulsed anew in my eyes as my armor perfected itself around me. My crystallized skin crackled with light as my rekindled sword hissed and whispered, silencing the plot of those who came against me. Above, below, to my left and right, they surrounded me. I flung myself in rage in all directions. My left hand rose and fell as power and Essence sliced through the ranks of the deceived. Blades crashed against my own. Some raked across my body, leeching Essence from my very core. My wrath fueled my sorrow as I slew one brother, only to watch another take his place. Thusly, we did battle.

I could hear the taunts of the enemy. "Do you see, *O Prince?* You have lost. Two? Against the Hosts? Are you mad, Miyka'el? Give in; all is lost." With no word or warning, a thunderclap ripped the sky. I knew Miyka'el answered the challenge with one of his own, though I could no longer see or hear him; I made thunder of my own.

In the sky, I created a breach in the shell of fallen brothers that surrounded me. The space allowed me time enough to soar swiftly above them all. I whirled high and wheeled around staring at the monsters clawing at my ascent. Wonder and sorrow gripped me, but both were soon replaced by wrath as I thought of what they were. As one they rose, as one they hunted me, and as one they would fall. I knew my own strength could no longer save me. With this in mind I prayed for faith. I turned again, roaring higher and higher above those that hunted me.

I turned as my raging eyes flared for a last moment while my weapon evaporated; I drew its used Essence back into me. Cupping my hands together, I called for strength as the amount Essence I wielded shook my very core. Power grew and welled up within me. I checked again to ensure that Miyka'el was safe and away from what I planned to unleash. The Hosts reached closer still, but not close enough. Power leaked from my own eyes as I tried to keep it in. Light burned through my skin; Essence squeezed from every pore. They were still not close enough, and I needed more.

My armor grew in size and brilliance. Light bled through as I continued to focus. My hands ached and my arms felt as if they would disintegrate. I rattled within the shell of armor I shaped, but still I held as my enemies came closer. Until the storm broke.

"Enough!" My cry did nothing to stop them. On they came. Screaming, tearing, raging. "*Enough!*" Again, nothing. They were almost upon me. "*Enough!*" Still, nothing. "*So be it,*" I whispered.

Light ripped from my outstretched hands. Essence roared from my armor, hair, and eyes. Those almost upon me crackled into nothingness as their very screams were torn from existence. Their eyes melted as they stared into my own. The beam traveled deep and unswerving all the way to the ground. Whatever it touched was destroyed. My brothers were torn asunder from their very shaping. Their abrupt screams haunt me still, but Miyka'el needed time. If Satan fell, the Hosts would soon follow suit.

Even though I destroyed an entire column, the Legions still stretched to both horizons of the Plains of Heaven. Weakness shackled me; my knees buckled and my wings shook, dimmer now than they were moments before. I glanced again to see how Miyka'el fared, but I could no longer see the battle. I guessed him to be on the opposite side of the Palace. Slowly, my thoughts faded, my vision blurred, an upper wing crumpled and twitched, and I fell from the sky.

IX

"How you have fallen from heaven, O morning star, son of the dawn!"

-Isaiah 14:12-

How long I lay after my fall I knew not. It could not have been for long, however, for those pursuing me had yet to strike at me before my senses returned. The Essence I released left the front line far enough back where I had time to recover. My dimmed, crackling blue eyes blinked and glanced around as I tried to find my Chief Prince. Oddly enough, I had fallen near the small hill where I had hidden at the beginning, back where I began.

My power fled, my crystallized skin became soft, my hair shortened, and my eyes remained dull. Any Essence I once held within me was unleashed against those I once loved. Even my armor softened and let go of its bindings, becoming robes once again. Thus weakened, I could only hide and wait.

Far out into the plain, I could see that the armies were reforming. The dark officers brought order back into the ranks. My breath began to slow and my vision corrected itself as Essence slowly snuck back into my broken body.

The silence gripping the battlefield seemed alien in the wake of the clash I witnessed moments before. I could still not find either Satan or Miyka'el. I glanced down to the steps of the Palace to see the still form of a dead friend caked in dust. The corpse rested amidst the bodies of the Fallen I had laid to rest around him. I assumed my own must soon join that pile, for I would not hide again.

With no weapon, armor, or power I descended that lonely hill and came unto the steps of the Palace. In a last gasp of a Shaping I formed in my hand a pathetic rendition of my first blade. My eyes slid shut in exhaustion as my breaths rasped through weakly clenched teeth. The sword shook in my hands, so I stuck it point first into the earth, leaning doggedly on the hilt while doing my best to appear otherwise. My last stand would be where Heaven's first was made.

The Legions gathered for a final time. There was no sign of Miyka'el. I thought I remembered glimpsing my Prince and our enemy railing against the other before my earlier ascension and the ensuing release of Essence. I could not have been unconscious but for a few moments, yet there came no sound, no challenge, and no indication of any battle taking place. The only noises that drifted across that still plain were those coming from the line of the enemy. I tried to ignore them while thinking where Satan and Miyka'el could be. From across the plain, there arose a cry, a scream to pierce the fading peace of silence.

Far across that vast expanse, amidst the traitors there arose a sound of rage, sorrow, and grief. The accursed noise, however, now fueled itself upon the depravity of Satan's immense malice. That which I heard but could not see thrashed through my imagination and tore at my sanity. What new madness was this? I knew too little to understand the evil taking place across that grassy expanse. It was the work of torture.

My core cringed at the sound while my eyes feverishly combed the expanse, struggling to find its source. What could make such a noise? There was no power in it, no hope, or joy—only despair and pain. I continued hearing the weak cry until a lone word broke clear across the sky, shattering my faith along with my courage.

"Father!!!"

My eyes gaped wide as my senses reeled back unto me, reclaiming the focus I previously lost. The sword shook in the ground as my grief caused my arms to convulse. My legs grew weak as I kneeled over the pommel. I rested my forehead on the grip as tears slid down to the point. I had found my Prince.

Those who once loved their Captain now tortured him for pleasure, forced to satisfy their perverse appetites. Open battle was an evil unto itself, but to issue pain on the broken seemed an empty practice for a dying race. I heard every cry, felt every gasp, and yet I stood motionless, helpless to silence them. Beelzebub knew my weakness, and through the screams of my Captain, my own torture commenced. I fell humbled to the dirt before the lifeless house of the Lord Our God, praying to a Father I thought I knew. If evil be our fate, how could we claim service to a loving God? If such madness ravished our perfection, who was to blame other than the one who fashioned it? Accusations grew in my head as prayers and petitions gathered alongside them in my mind, yet there came no answers.

Tears stuck to my face and spittle draped itself from my lips to my sword. Moist eyes raised themselves again to scan that scarred field. All was dead. Then, off in the distance, silhouetted against the sky a lone form arose. It hung small in the sky, yet grew in size as it came ever closer. I wiped my glowing eyes and began to stand. I realized I still used my pathetic saber for a crutch, so I stubbornly yanked it from the ground as the form continued to approach.

I could soon ascertain that it was actually two figures which came to me, but only two wings carried them. Horror flashed across my face before I managed to compose myself. I would not let this perversion destroy whatever pride, power, or faith I had left to harbor. Then they were upon me.

A giant crashed into the ground. I had no idea who he was. I had never seen him before, or whatever I knew of him was completely lost in my mind. Dark hair, taut as wires stretched around his head and shoulders like an unkempt mane. His eyes seemed empty and dark, like the abysmal incarnation of what Satan longed to establish. *Darkness.* There was no light, only the absence thereof. Blood red fire curled softly from his eyes without heat or glow. The rest of his face was a shadow of distortions that I could not see. A black, lightless cape slid from his back to the ground and the crimson underside kicked up rogue earth as he strode from the sky. Hardened casing which seemed more a void of nothingness than armor, adorned itself down the being's torso. Evil signs and symbols slid all over his armor, and his legs were encased in beryl, which showed the blackness of his skin beneath.

In his right hand, coils of chain ending in an extended sickle were loosely wrapped, and in his left hung the limp form of our Archangel. The creature gripped Miyka'el's neck. Liquid Essence poured from the Prince's unconscious eyes. The same issued from his gaping mouth, and some dripped from the grip wrapping round his neck. I swallowed my last tears and turned with what little pride I harbored towards that which had brought Heaven's only hope dangling in his hands.

"Who are you, Prince of Naught, to touch that which commands a love you have forgotten? Who are you to dare tread where you were breathed forth? Answer, or I will throw you from this holy Mount."

A black, blobbing growth sneaked from his closed lips and rolled over itself before a deep boom broke from his cavernous throat, shattering my weak words. *"Apollyon... That is what... you are to call me, Lesser."* A deep breath sucked into the shadow of his face before he spoke again. *"You would... be wise to never forget that... which I have taken. For such things will... be demanded of you, Servant of a Lightless Lamp. I am... Son of the Devil... Keeper of Things to Come... Remember me, Kaos, for I will... have you."*

X

With a deep, guttural snarl he hurled the Third at my shaking feet. Essence leaked from Miyka'el's numerous wounds; his wings bent backwards, all wrong and twisted. His hair hung damp and clung to his ashen face while all his armor was stripped of him; only a loose conglomeration of soiled, torn robes remained draped over his dying frame. My pride kept still my tears as my last hope, Heaven's last hope, lay broken at my feet. My soul cringed in sorrow and despair, yet there remained nothing left for which to weep? No, I would not cry.

"You, Dread Prince, have brought your lifeless offering. Now return your own carcass to the grave that vomited your presence before me. My eyes grow weary looking on your face, or what remains of it."

The shadow marring my opponent's visage deepened then pulsed as echoed laugher thrummed from the deep recesses of the creature's being. His head rose in the briefest of moments before his fiery eyes riveted themselves upon me once again. And I knew fear.

"Soon... Lesser. Soon, I will... come for you, but now... the Master

of the House… wishes for you to bear witness to what… he shall establish. Then, I… will break you."

Before I could respond, he simply rose into the sky, and with one jerk of his wings he was away. As soon as I was certain he turned from me, I collapsed over my Captain. I gently turned his face to the sky and pushed the clinging hair from his face. I had too little Essence to use, so I sat still before my fallen savior.

"Miyka'el? Miyka'el!? Arise! They have not claimed you—could not have claimed you! Miyka'el!" There came no answer. The Captain of the Hosts rested silently in front of our Father's closed gates. Suddenly, from across the field there came a note. A threat and a promise carried violently on the winds, on the blast of a horn.

I cradled Miyka'el's head in my arms; Novation lay a spear length behind me, and I, in the midst of our stricken trinity, was the only one left to lament. The thunder of footsteps carried damnation across the field and certainty took captive my faith. We were lost. The Father of Lies, the God I once trusted, stayed buried deep within the caverns of his palace. *God is dead or He is a coward.* My heart fought my mind and my beliefs scrapped for survival as logic demanded proof. Wherever He was it was not here; I envied Him, dead or alive.

"K—Kaos…"

My eyes flashed to the Third as his own trembled open.

"Miyka'el? I thought you lost!"

"Not yet. Have faith, Son of God. Remember yourself; He is watching."

"Miyka'el, it's over. They're coming to destroy everything." I hated speaking of the traitor as if he controlled out fate, but it felt at times as if he did. "We are broken. I have nothing left to offer the fight, and the cause I knew before leaves me little left for which to fight."

"That was never your command!" Miyka'el's snapping bark ended in a cough as it broke my whimpering. Essence spluttered down his faded chin. "You are ordered… to fight! No matter the cause… or cost. You must lay it down... I have not failed; I have obeyed. When the greatest among us... are humbled... then He exalts... Himself. Watch, and bear witness... to such sovereignty as His."

As the last of his words fled from his bleeding mouth, his strained chest and eyes grew still and calm. He laid lifeless in my arms with only faint warmth left to assure me he was alive. My eyes burned as I laid my hero's head down into the dirt for which he fought.

I sat numb, unmoving, for a scant moment in Time before I began to rage.

"Is *this* your great plan, my great God!? Father, Abba, how great you must be to craft such a wonderful Creation! *Look!* Behold your work, Father! Look at the creativity, the beauty. *Father* on High, praise be to *your* name, Great One! Let not us mar *your* perfection, for it seems we can not manage ourselves!" My wings, limp and pale as they were, flashed and fluttered in fury against God.

How could He? After all I, we, had strived to become, *this*... this was our Fate. I would not and could not accept it as such. "*You! You* are the one who crafted us! *Your* imperfection scarred what we could have been! If there was no evil, from where did it come, since *you* created all things? *You,* it came from *you,* Great Deceiver! Now, as I sit prepared to die for *you,* I realize that you would never dare to die for me!" As I screamed towards the silence of the Throne, a stray thought ran through my mind. *As the Son becomes the Father, so the Father becomes the Son.* I do not know from where it came, but I quickly smothered it in hatred.

Exhausted, I fell next to the Third. Tears mixed with my Essence and dripped from my face. My wings twitched in the dirt as dust leapt round my hands. My hair clamped wet and thick to my sickly scalp. My torn robes shifted and cracked from the liquid that dried on them. I hid my face in my hands for a short moment before I fell down between my heroes, trying to forget what brought us here.

XI

My eyes rested shut. The distant tempo and thunder of the army approaching became a distant murmur, mingled with the pulse of my vanishing life. I no longer cared, and the sweet sleep of apathy washed over my crippled state as we three lay ruined before the home of a God.

A crack like that of a whip crashed through the valley. Ears ringing, I hastily stumbled up, turning to look at the doors. The tall, monolithic portal of the Palace that remained unmoving for so long now trembled violently. It shook with thunderous rumbles as something within pushed it open.

I could not move. Fear shackled my legs and paralyzed my thoughts. Had judgment come at last? It no longer mattered. With death before me and damnation behind I could not run, so I stared and beheld the birth of my humiliation.

The doors slammed outwards against the walls of the palace, spraying debris in all directions. My eyes ached from the brilliance that sliced through the air, but I willed them to remain open. The scene slowly settled as the light faded with it. Glancing inside, I saw—Nothing. It was not as if I did not see what I expected to see, or even the absence of light, for I would have called it Darkness. What I saw was Nothing, a blackness that lacked darkness while desiring light, and a chaos that possessed order I accepted as indiscernible. That is all I saw, until they walked out.

At first, they seemed small, insignificant. They were nothing more than lights playing in my eyes, but what seemed insignificant soon crippled my spirit. Seven, seven of them in all walked forth from the Nothing.

Each shrouded their faces in deep, dark hoods that held light in as well as kept it out, for embedded deep in those cowls were visages that bore two piercing blue lights. *Eyes.* Bright, wrathful eyes stared down at me. Their dark robes, which knew neither color nor light, swayed round their damning steps as they came still closer. Cavernous sleeves hid arm and hand as they were joined together near the creatures' chests. I saw nothing of those that wore these dark clothes, but they did speak, and I did listen.

"Who are you, unmade clay, to question the workings of the Almighty? You lament against which you do not know. You rage against your only hope. His story was penned as you first knew breath, yet here you wail, as if your words could challenge the ways of His Will. *Behold!* A new order is being established. Remain silent and bear witness. His glory you will exalt, and your will shall be His will." They spoke in one voice, harmonic throughout in perfect unison.

Across the plains marched the Legions, endless and seemingly unscathed by the damage my Captain and I sought to inflict. Apollyon, the offspring of perversion, marched at their head. A step ahead paced his maker, the taint of heaven, Beelzebub. From where I sat I could feel the pounding of their steps, sending shivers and tremors through the foundation of Heaven.

As I watched the approaching force, the Seven came before us.

Behind, the doors gaped wide unto the same emptiness I beheld before. The end was nigh upon us, and I had cursed my Savior.

"Bring the Lord Captain and the little one up to the steps. Keep them close. If they leave your side, or more likely, if you leave theirs, we can no longer guarantee the same safety we offer now." Again as one, they spoke. I soundlessly obeyed, still not knowing who or what they were.

Miyka'el slumped to my right while Novation lay crumpled to my left. I started to stand, but one of the Seven spoke out. "You should kneel, and pray for this day. It grows dark, unknown, even unto our eyes. It appears He keeps His Will from us as well. Pray Child... pray."

My eyes held questions I knew they would ignore, but I kneeled nevertheless, giving voice to my thoughts in hopes my Father could still hear his prodigal son over the thunder in the plains. Soon the storm would break, and this time, there would be no reserve, only destruction. Seven stood against the Fallen legion. What is faith against such things?

Our Guardians did not move, but waited motionless as they stood semi-circled in front of us. Their dark robes offered no answers to their identity. They were lights, shrouded in their own darkness, and hidden away from Heaven itself. Only the blue light of their eyes betrayed their power as faint auras glowed on the ground before them. The pale, blue hue soon glowed in all directions, away from the three of us.

A figure rose from the oncoming Legion, and I instantly identified the same dark shape that brought my broken Captain back to me. Yet this time, others came with him. Six joined him in the air and they soon raced timeless across the sky and blinked into stillness only a short distance from our Circle. There existed a moment of breathless anticipation, until the Seven before me made a challenge. Before, their voices rang in harmony and beauty, but now they hissed with a venomous threat.

"You dare to challenge the King. Until now the test was issued. Those who failed and those who succeeded have been sifted, and the perversions have been found, and thus shall be purged."

Apollyon's thick voice coughed on its own slime as liquid filth dripped from his maw. *"HA-HA-Hollow words... doorkeeper. Do you think... we have come... ignorant of what waits before us? Your end is near—and it shall be my hand that ushers you—into the darkness."*

A flash and Apollyon's taloned trunk of an arm lashed out towards the first of the Seven. The six with him shot forward as well. All fell into chaos. The attack froze with seven shimmering, immeasurably bright hands clutching at the claws of Apollyon and his minions. The Seven stood rigid, still holding their enemies in their grip as I turned to watch the one holding Apollyon, whose snatching claw dripped crimson Essence upon a hand that beamed with holiness incarnate. Fingers interlocked and palms shook as each squeezed the other. The eyes of my Guardian fluttered closed as the light dimmed, and then he spoke alone.

"If you knew my name, Beast, you would consider wisely the consequences of rising against me a second time. We are the Seven Names of God, only those which He would have you know. To know the Names Unspoken would tear asunder your very existence. I am El Shaddai! My mercy is fled! You are damned for beholding the name I have spoken."

El Shaddai, still clinging to Apollyon, dropped his hood as blue light lanced into the beast he held. Apollyon's face singed as the Guardian brought his second hand to bear upon the creature's chest. A rippling shockwave flew from the hand as Satan's Son hurled backwards, skipping and skidding along the ground until he came to rest nearby. Alongside, the Seven slammed their assailants violently to the earth. I heard several loud snaps, and none of them rose.

I thought the blow to Apollyon must have crushed him, but as soon as he stopped, that wiry black head shot upwards and those twin orbs of hate stared at the ten of us. In a blink he stood. Smoke sizzled from his face and energy crackled along his chest as he slowly walked toward us a second time. The strength of Shaddai shocked me. If this creature aided in felling Miyka'el, how could one of the Seven have humbled him so? As powerful as the blast seemed, however, Apollyon seemed unhindered in his resilience. Pure hatred burned in his eyes, and it did not dim.

He stopped five paces away, his gaze panning over our faces and his stricken servants, finally resting on El Shaddai. "*I would tell you—I have a message—for your Master, but it appears—He has forsaken you. You have but to—march on the traitor, and—my Maker will yet forgive you—possibly.*" Black skin twitched and flexed under his opaque armor.

"*Your words are a forgotten wind, traitor. Do your Maker's imps dare cross this threshold? Hold to your fading lies and see what burning wrath falls on your ruined state!*" Shaddai's voice thundered into echoes and drifted on into silence. All was still, until Shaddai spoke again, "*Tell your bastard father of what I have said. Tell him I stand here, awaiting the return of the Second, so that I may cast him down. Forgiveness is truly lost.*" He drew his hood forward, folded his hands within his robes, and became still.

Apollyon fumed, wreaking forth the foulness of his breath, and I briefly thought he would attack again. He turned, however, and with a cry that screeched all around he flew back to the place from which he came.

A calm fell upon Heaven.

XII

I sat paralyzed, gazing into the ground. Apollyon disappeared into the traitorous ranks that halted a short distance away. Miyka'el and Novation still motionless beside me, I slowly rose to my knees, kneeling as I purveyed the Seven that stood before me. All was silent; they stood without word or movement.

The authority with which our Guardians dispatched Apollyon granted me a momentary respite from my doubts. The Son of the Traitor, however, was but one, albeit powerful, entity. There remained a myriad of angels left fresh for the final assault. I felt neither ease nor peace, even with these powerful allies sent before us. *Where was God?* Whether angels or beings bearing His very name came to our aid, they were not God and could not replace Him.

The Legions poised silently, but that would soon change, bringing wrath unto the Halls of God. So many unknowns, so much loss poisoned my hope. I looked down the corpse of my closest friend, now grimed with soil and Essence that caked his delicate features. Novation's dark eyes stared into the Nothing we would all become.

Such was my fear: that I would return to that which I once was. Such fears stayed with me, reminding me of what I should never become.

My thoughts halted as the drumbeats of my brothers' feet boomed across the plains separating our small band from their own inevitable eternity. They were coming, and I would no longer kneel. Shaddai turned as he saw me rise. *"Child, you cannot fight this fight. The battle is not yours, but the Lord's. Who will save you if you damn yourself now?"*

"I have grown tired of fear, Bright One. You may see the Face of God, but such luxuries are now denied to those in this world. Until I see Him again, I have only faith, and that will either sustain me or betray me. My hope may become my greatest traitor, or greatest victory. Do not deny me my last freedom; I despair in that I have but one eternity to lose for my Father, if Father he still is." My words echoed through my mind as their implications burned meaning into my actions.

"As you wish, but what is yet to be seen you know not of."

I raised my small sword and stood near the Seven while the rest of Heaven's Host marched ever closer. Doubts rushed through me. *Why stand?* There may yet be hope. *Why suffer needlessly against those who imprisoned a God with the fear of their own strength?* I cannot fear. My own deeds defined me, and soon their consequence would be demanded of me. I hoped such things would keep me from the cowardice that constricted my comfort while compelling me to combat the Fallen, even if I found myself falling alongside them.

My thoughts silenced themselves as the Legions came upon us. The Seven did not move as they gazed at the Enemy. My saber shook in my raised grip, legs gliding into a guarded stance while my feet shifted for balance. The thunder roared around us as Satan's host bellowed in rage against the existence they were given. Hope faded and still the Seven stood silent. Madness ringed around us, piercing our ears with blasphemous roars and evil cries. My eyes roamed, looking for a weakness, a break in their line, or an edge by which to turn the tide, but there were none. I could only stand, and brace myself for the end.

Over the din, I heard a different cry. A softer note carried on countless voices streaming over the Gates came from behind. My eyes riveted on my enemies, but my ears followed those grace-ful notes. It happened all at once. The ranks lurched to a halt as their eyes flew to look at what came from behind me. Their bellow silenced and the clear note took up prominence. Risking a glance, I turned and saw the turn of the tide, flying over the walls of the Palace. Brothers all, their angelic forms cascaded over our broken few, charging into the bewildered damned.

Following their flight with my eyes, I heard their note turn to a roar as the music for which they were made to create grew silent under the chaos of war. Without a warrior among them, they charged into their doom, for theirs was the way of song and praise.

As they poured endlessly onto the field, they eventually out-numbered the Legions they opposed. Thousands of wings flared wide as their bearers clashed with the Fallen. With voices meant for song and with hands meant solely for worship, they bellowed and fought against the perversion of Heaven. Essence flowed onto the plains as my brothers died.

The ranks closed, battle was joined, and Essence continued to flash and pour near the Gates of the Throne. They were the remain-der of Heaven, who were neither chosen nor corrupted by the lies of our Fallen Prince.

XIII

*"His tail swept a third of the stars our of the sky
and flung them to the earth."*

-Revelation 12:4-

Essence flashed and fell over the battle as crushed entities crawled in their own filth. Wounds gushed, coating the ground with a crystal colored liquid that flowed over the hilts of Heaven's murderers. Madness gripped the battle as the sheer numbers of the angelic reinforcements threatened to overwhelm the hosts of the rebels. My eyes burned with the power that exploded before them as white fire soon raged along the lengths of the swarm. The initial roar turned to screams as bodies fell countless from the smoking sky, while the ground soon held piles of the dead. The corpses were scorched black with the perverted Essence used to destroy those we were never meant to lose.

The losses of both forces piled over the plain as the initial surprise of the Lessers' attack faded from the Enemy. The lines held steady, however, even as the bloody faces contorted in pain, more intense for being felt for the first time. I stood helpless before the remains of my friend and the motionless form of my captain. One gone, the other seemingly so, our broken alliance sat rimmed by the Seven standing circled around us. As far as I could see to both right and left, screams echoed toward me from the stretched ranks, yet the Lessers held. Wrought only for worship and the tender necessities of art and song, they still fought for a Father I believed lost. Their faith held the fighting at bay, until the Deceiver arose against them.

Rising from the midst of the battle, a dark, writhing shape convulsed in the air. I peered out into a fading sky, knowing immediately the Prince who was hovering menacingly over the forces below him. He flew while simultaneously transforming. *For the last time,* I prayed before I realized who I was beseeching. Hopelessness draws out faith, especially when belief is all we have left to grasp.

The fighting slowed, giving the Lessers an opportunity to glance above at their traitorous lord, who now sat ringed in a blue fire smothering his face and all his features. Fear gripped the Lessers while apprehension flowed through the rebels, waiting to see their lord's new strength. The hiss of the flames could be heard over the field as silence gripped the countless. His body scorched and scarred over; I could not determine whether this was part of Beelzebub's plan or some form of final annihilation. Perhaps Sin was finally destroying its host. I stared along with the others, until an explosion ripped wide the sky and flung the legions from their feet.

Leathery wings flew from the source of the explosion, each black and smothered with an oily, red liquid that dripped sizzling into the ground where it fell. Soon, horrifically smoke-scarred legs, each coated in metallic plates and scales grew from the light that sat blaring in the midst of this transformation. Talons and claws clicked and gleamed from the tips of these armored appendages. Then the body, cavernous from within and titanic without, stretched and snapped into existence as the interior of the monster took its final shape. A long, powerful, sinuous neck snaked upward from the body, perched upon shoulders shuddering with Essence. Then the head, flaring in flames and coated in its own wrath, took shape. Venom trickled from the gaping jaws while yellow, madness-gripped eyes bulged with hatred and agony. Teeth the size of spears gnashed and clanged threats upon the field. Such was the first Dragon.

XIV

"…And the dragon and his angels fought back."

-Revelation 12:7-

Eyes wide with fear I looked to the Seven who stood unmoving in their ever steady circle. Those facing away from the roars screeching from across the field never turned to see their source. The lines of Lessers faltered, falling back in fear from the monstrous drake flinging fire into the heavens. Many, cut down from behind, fell as they fled back towards where I crouched. Terror spread throughout our army, causing the line to bend then break. From the sky as well as the ground there fled a host of my brothers.

My eyes watched a small niche remaining behind. All of them soaked in Essence, gleaming in their own brilliance, none of them ever meant to carry a blade, charged into the midst of the enemy. The Legions fell around them. One of ours, a youthful looking Lesser with shining blue hair rose into the sky, flashes of thunder and Essence falling from his body. Explosions lashed into the Enemy ranks, before a black beam tore him asunder as he fell from the air.

Those remaining, several hundred or so, formed a sphere of blades and wings. They appeared as a stone in the middle of a raging river. Small screams of defiance tore from their midst as the remnants of their broken army fled past our position. Eventually, a dark, monstrous demon lord swayed up to their barricade. With a lash of a whip he tore a dozen from their ranks, the whip lacerating them into bloody masses. A group in the middle of the sphere reformed and assaulted him. A black blade flashed into existence and fell upon them. Their sacrifice fell wet onto the earth as the others flinched; I was sure they would break. In a last surge, however, one brave individual, smaller than the rest, rose up a cry I could not hear, and the whole force of the remnant fell upon that one lord. Letting their guard down from the demons to the side and behind them, they quickly began to fall. Yet as the last few died on the field, I watched a gleaming bright flash tear itself into the neck of their adversary, and the dark lord fell gurgling onto the mass of those who sacrificed themselves, a fading blade stuck deep under his gaping jaws.

In flight and on foot, the decimated Lessers continuously dashed past us. They fought for so short a time, but at least they made their stand. Their faces full of horror, they flew to the heights of the Temple while some fell stricken below the Gates. To the left and right, I could see the vanguards flying back to us, seeking shelter in the only place left for hope—the Throne of their God.

The Seven moved. I gazed up from my pity and watched these beings mobilize. *Why did they wait? So many dead—so many.* El Shaddai slowly drew back his hood, allowing blue light to simmer around us as he turned towards the center of our circle. Behind him, Satan's army seethed and raged, coming closer, while their new leader, the Dragon, came behind. There was no fear in the eyes of El Shaddai. Crackling with Essence, he spoke, *"Whom do We serve?"*

Wondering whether or not to speak, I glanced around my motionless guardians, preparing my answer. Then one by one, every member of the Seven, ending with El Shaddai, gave their powerful response while simultaneously removing their hoods.

"*Elohim.*"

"*Adonai.*"

"*Kurios.*"

"*Ikanos.*"

"*Jehovah-Jireh.*"

"*Je-Hoshua.*"

"*El Shaddai.*"

"*Under these names We shall battle.*" Shaddai turned, eyes burning with vengeance and wrath at the armies decrying his God. Brilliance flamed bright through his being as his robe fell from his frame, along with those of the Six others. Light flashed as Satan's host briefly stumbled, pausing in their march. Only the Dragon did not slow.

Far to the sides, the rebel hosts squeezed tight their formation, condensing in front of the natural bottleneck fronting the Gates. They formed a staggeringly endless column stretching far past the voluminous legs of their perverted leader. In this manner they marched, coming closer to the feet of the Seven.

Shaddai reached out his hand, palm open to the sky, as explosions began to echo above him. Masses of dark mists congealed overhead, covering the battlefield in a hazy cover of lightless chaos. Shaddai clenched his fist, and lightning fell from the heavens and struck him where he stood.

Wings, encased in some shimmering, viscous armor, shot from his shoulders, his back, and his hips. Six total, sprang into the air, along with the wings of the others. The Seven flamed in a brilliant blue blaze that seared white to my eyes as Adonai roared.

Erupting in Essence, the first of the Seven slammed his hands flat to the ground, sending seismic rumbles out from his palm. His eyes closed, shading his brilliance for an instant before they sprang open while a roar tore from his lips. He jerked his hands into the air, and as he did I noticed the green light connecting his hands with the ground. The tinted Essence leaped into the Seven, swirling into each of them as their blue flame merged with the latter. All Seven hunched over as in pain, and as one reared up against the sky, throwing their arms wide as they screamed in perfect unison the names of our God.

"*Shaddai! Elohim! Adonai! Kurios! Ikanos! Jehovah-Jireh! Je-Hoshua!*" The names roared across the ranks now marching slightly slower than before. As they continued, however, the Seven continued to change.

The green and blue flame merged, coalescing into a brilliant, shard covered armor. Flame and light danced in their hair; Essence crackled, sizzling in their eyes; the crystalline armor molded to their arms and legs; the light once emanating from their bodies now pulsed and shimmered over their armored forms.

The demonic army moved closer, the front lines wary in their approach, yet confident in their numbers. Sinister weapons hung from the hands of every one while madness gripped their eyes. The Dragon roared.

The Seven moved forward, forming a line in front of me and the Gates. They harbored no doubt. They merely stood, wings spread wide so as to shield the Throne from the profane armies coming to its very steps.

Slowly, Shaddai lowered his head, closed his eyes, and breathed a whisper unto the Seven, "*To War…*"

XV

As one they moved. Stepping forward with each right hand hovering over the ground, the Seven stared down the approaching legions. I heard snarls and snaps as my fallen brothers came nearer. I looked around at the Seven, wondering how they could possibly stand against the armies of heaven itself.

The thunder from the Legions' approach pounded closer, until the deafening roar of their charge drowned out my last scream before chaos erupted all around me.

"*Abba!*" Shaddai's scream roared into Satan's ranks as he raised his right hand into the air brandishing an illuminated shield, cast in brilliant white light. The others did likewise, poising their left hands to the sides of their tall, tower shields. In a flaring moment of heat and fire, I saw long, shimmering spears form in the hands of the Seven.

The first ranks of the hosts closed in, driven by maddening hatred. The Seven, as one, spears outthrust from between their shields, merely stepped into the horde that fell upon them.

Spear points lurched and bit into the first that approached the

Seven. Throats split and Essence gurgled and pooled around the bases of the shields planted firmly in the ground. Beams of light extended from the spearheads, tearing gaping holes through rank after rank of dark brothers. The long weapons gashed wounds into the attackers whose weapons could neither outreach nor parry the ferocity of Shaddai and the Names.

The Enemy vanguard to my right attempted to come around and engulf the Guardians where they stood, until Adonai reared back with his spear and sent it thundering into the ground at their feet. Several dozen of the attackers' legs instantly incinerated as dust and earth flew high into the air, showering the ranks coming behind.

Lighting smoked from Adonai's eyes as he held his hand again to the sky. A long, curved blade, etched in holy runes of an unknown tongue, appeared in his grasp. Veering from the group, he strode out to face the remaining brothers who pushed over the sides of the narrow entryway.

As Adonai engaged the Fallen, I glanced to the left and saw another group breaking around the Seven. Ikanos flung his spear into the ranks approaching in front, skewering four of the Fallen who fell gutted on his weapon, before he launched into the sky. Pitching left, he came around behind the advancing ranks, eyes searing with a white flame. As he flew over the rear ranks they attempted to cry a warning to the demon lord in their vanguard, who turned just in time to see Ikanos slam the base of his shield into his exposed neck. Ikanos drove the shield straight through to the ground, thrusting the lord off his feet as his neck broke and splintered on the earth.

Spinning quickly, Adonai turned his shield so it reached down the length of his arm. In rage he roared as it burned bright with bluish fire. Essence sizzled and dripped from the ruptured eyes of the Fallen who failed to avert their eyes in time. The ones behind covered their gaze, cowering behind those with seared eyes who spun and tripped, falling over each other in their blindness. Ikanos again lowered his shield to the ground, watching the smoldered and burnt faces wander over the field.

The battle raged as the Five in the middle held off the main charge. Essence flashed and crashed on the shields as the weapons of the enemy broke and shattered on their brilliance. Screams leapt from both sides as the Names held their place and the Fallen died at their feet.

From behind the front ranks, a wave of enemy ranks soared high into the air. They surged forward, meaning to overwhelm the Names from above and behind. Just as the crest of this wave broke upon the Names, the Enemy reared back, all of them simultaneously forming short, sharpened, spear-like instruments in their upheld hands. *Javelins.*

The sharp weapons fell by the dozens upon the Five still striving to hold the middle. All of the Names quickly raised their shield, the javelins glancing off to the right and left. My sword arm shook as I watched the javelins splinter on the shields a short distance in front of me. I lowered my gaze, watching for any of the Fallen who could threaten my stricken brothers. I failed to notice, however, as a lone traitor crawled over the bodies of the dead lying in front of the Names. Just as the shields were raised into the air, I heard Kurios scream in pain and turn, seething as he spun to the one who wounded him. The lone soldier whimpered as Kurios' fury burned in his eyes, the enemy's sword still sticking from below his left arm. With a quick snarl, he tore the sword from his side, and deftly sliced off the head cowering in terror before him.

Shaddai, seeing Kurios wounded, quickly cried out to the Names. *"Stay the hand! Fall back! To Kurios!"* The Five in the middle formation swarmed Kurios, whose eyes burned in anger and pain. The enemies above now dove down, swords and pikes replacing the absent javelins, and they were led by a grimacing Fallen whose size looked far greater than the rest. Roaring, flame leapt from the great one's eyes as he dove down. Elohim glanced at the descending horde, knowing they could not both care for Kurios and hold them off without more loss. *"Shaddai! Take the Names to the Gate; I'll buy you the time you need!"*

Shaddai glanced quizzically at his Brother, and then he understood. Turning to Kurios, whose Essence leaked out onto the Field, he quickly spun back to Elohim, knowing what must be done. *"Go Brother. May our Names' Sake guide you back to us."*

Elohim closed his eyes; hot drops of Essence fell from his face before turning to the angels still falling towards them. *"Not my Will..."* Bellowing in holy wrath Elohim screamed into the sky, his shield falling to the ground below. Hundreds of the Fallen screeched towards him, hate glowing in their eyes and Essence fueling their vengeance.

Right as they fell upon him, Elohim splintered his own armor allowing it to also fall to the earth below. Spinning past the first rank of blades, he charged into the midst of the host in the heavens, completely exposed as he came to a stop in between two of his enemy. His hands launched sideways to each of their faces, glowing in a faint light as each one came palm up next to their targets. Before either of the Fallen could respond, Essence burned from Elohim's hands and reduced both their heads to ashes. I saw the quick flash of light, watched as two of the lost brothers fell headless from the sky, heard Elohim scream as they filled him with their blades, and gasped as an explosion ripped through the heavens.

Lightning scorched through the ranks above as each wound the Fallen had gashed into Elohim discharged uncontrollably burning chaos into his enemies. I turned my head and covered Miyka'el's as the seething light burned the ground around us. The light began to fade before I dared look back into the sky. There, poised above us, hung Elohim, arms outstretched to either side, his frame frozen where he unleashed his wrath. Nothing remained of those he slew. Where hundreds were moments before, now only one of the Names remained.

As I watched, all light left Elohim's body, and his faded, evanescent corpse fell from where he hung in the sky, thudding to the ground within the midst of our enemies. From where I huddled, I could hear their gurgling cries of glee and perversion. I looked at Shaddai in time to see him wipe his moist eyes as he brought Kurios closer to where I stood.

Seeing Elohim's display of power, the advancing lines fell back and regrouped, giving Adonai and Ikanos time to retreat. The Six now gathered around me, laying Kurios beside Miyka'el.

Essence dripped from his mouth and soaked the underside of his armor, but his stern eyes assured me he was not finished.

Looking into the distance, I heard Satan roar as flames jumped skyward. I watched as his sinuous neck snapped back, his jaws flinging a small, limp form, with lifeless legs and arms, high into the air before he snatched it to himself with his bloody maw.

Thus perished Elohim.

XVI

"I AM WHO I AM."

-Exodus 3:14-

The horror of Elohim's death gripped us all. Shaddai, standing aside from us scanned the swirling mass of the Fallen preparing to come at the Throne. His wings twitched and convulsed with fury and grief. Lightning sizzled and split from his feet into the earth. Jireh slowly panned his hands over Kurios' side and face. Light glowed from his hands as his brother's visage relaxed and the tension from his wounds left his body.

I felt helpless, lost. Even after resting for so long, I had regained little strength. Miyka'el began to stir, but his moans hinted little at his regaining consciousness. The sky seemed darker while below, the Legions amassed in ranks once again.

Ikanos must have perceived my worry. *"Do not doubt. This day is unfinished, and there is much left unknown to us all."*

I slowly nodded while I forced myself to walk on shaky legs to where Shaddai stood. I cautiously approached, not wanting to interrupt his meditations so soon after losing Elohim, yet before I could speak he called me by name.

"Kaos."

I brushed damp hair from my forehead as I responded, "Yes, Shaddai?"

"Of all the things ever told us by our God, which were the greatest of His Truths?"

Truth? What is Truth? Truth was dead alongside the One who created it. "I am no longer a witness to any Truth left to follow, Lord. All is waste, and ruin." I never before considered the question. Such things were as they were. Unquestionable absolutes of our existence were never meant to be contradicted nor rivaled, until Satan opposed all we ever knew. I feared my answer would anger Shaddai, but he gave no implication that he was.

"You still doubt. Look past what you are; behold what you were."

Confusion crumbled my thoughts as I grasped at his meaning. "I do not understand. I am what I am, as I always have been."

"Yet you cannot see while you flee who you are. You are weakness, shelled in the temporal nature of your current self, broken so that you can heal, abandoned so that you can redeem, alone so that you can perish."

"Perish?! Then there is no hope!"

"Not for who you currently are. No."

"Then *why* am I? I can do nothing; they are too powerful, too many."

"You fear death?" Shaddai interrupted.

"I—yes, I fear death, even though I know nothing of it. All I know it to be is a loss. We lose those in death even as those left to us continue to fade."

"Yes. Everything is fading. The Old Ways are changing. It is no longer safe to love. You always lose what you love, yes?"

It was a simple a question. My eyes hesitantly looked to Novation, at his still face and small, still arms. My vision blurred as I recalled my friend's sacrifice. I failed them all. My role, so brief and insignificant, was truly meaningless in comparison to the works of the Names of God, and their more faithful servants.

"Why, Shaddai? It should have been me? It should always have been me!" Fists slammed the ground, raking over the dried, sharp stones. Essence flowed over them before I realized I was bleeding.

"Guilt is not of God, nor is shame."

I looked up from my bleeding hands. My body shook with grief. Down below us, horns blared in preparation for the assault. Not much time—never enough time. I glanced around in a hopeless daze.

"Did your friend die for your self-pity?"

The question barely registered, though it was enough for me to shake my head.

"For what did He die, aside for His God, aside for His faith?"

I hated myself, my weakness, my hesitation, my words, my thoughts; I hated Novation for dying for what I hated. I hated the Faith. For what did Novation die? In my mind, I heard his words again, resounding in my ears as if he had just spoken them aloud. *"By His strength I shall see you plummet; by my hand or by the one who even now is watching!"* The one watching, where I hid on a hill, and watched him die.

"No—he could not have; he would not have.

"Greater love has no one than this, that he lay down his life for his friends."

"Please, no more, Shaddai."

"He died for love."

Despite my guilt and self-loathing, in the midst of my weakness, Novation had laid down his life. I could no longer allow myself the luxury of guilt.

"There will be consequences for what has occurred today. To love anything in this world, to hold onto it, to cherish it, whether it be good or bad, will always lead to pain. We lose it all, Kaos. Only after this do we see."

"See what?"

"*That we must let go.*"

I cradled my face in my hands, rubbing my eyes as I tried to answer. "I don't know how."

"*Novation did. It was his love, not for himself, but for his brother, that allowed him to let go. Your friend is not resting in that corpse on the stair. He is elsewhere.*"

"What is there besides this? This is real, what was made. We cannot leave the border. This is the end."

"*The end? No, Kaos. Death is another step. A road we all must take because of what Satan has done. But I have seen what lies on the other side, little brother.*"

I looked up quizzically.

"*All the pains of this place will fade, and the miry veil between this place and the next pulls aside.*" He glanced skyward, inhaling deeply before turning to me again. "*Then you feel it.*"

I waited. "Feel what?"

"*That you've come home, as if things have been made right. And He will welcome every one who comes. There will be no more tears, no more pain.*"

"How do you find this place?"

"*You will know. Sometimes the road is narrow, other times it is wide, but there is only one portal to enter upon it. You will come to know more of this.*"

I studied Novation over near the steps, wondering what he was seeing, where he was going, hoping Shaddai spoke the truth.

"*Will you believe, Son of God?*"

I turned from the body of my friend as I nodded.

"*Then perhaps you should stand up.*"

XVII

"You have forgotten God your Savior; you have not
remembered the Rock, your fortress."

-Isaiah 17:10-

Shaddai walked back to the other Five as I sat pondering over what Shaddai spoke to me. I no longer held any power, yet he expected me to arise alongside the others. Confused, anxious, and still exhausted, I slowly walked back to where the others stood and kneeled, all eyes on the Enemy as they planned their next attack.

I looked behind them, to the Lessers still clustering in terrified groups around the doors to the Throne. Although most had fled far past the Gates, some still held hope that their salvation lay with the One contained within His Palace walls.

They all seemed lost, unsure of what would become of their reality, turning their kind faces in all directions as if trying to find answers in the air. Glancing to the front as I stood, I took in the frothing madness grouped not far from where we waited.

Insane faces, elongated fangs, eyes twisted and cruel, the manifestations of Satan's perverted use of Essence took effect on his army. No beauty remained in him or his followers. Ranks reformed, weapons were readied, and as I watched, Satan reared back titanic wings of indescribable size, opened wide his gory jaws, and roared, streaking flames and hate towards the direction of the Throne. They would come soon.

As I reached the Six, Jireh pointed to the host preparing their approach. "We must strike at them before they reach us. Direct melee will not avail us for long, not against that number."

"But remember, Brother. We only fight for time, not victory. Whichever method provides the greatest delay will be our means of warfare," replied Je-Hoshua.

"Perhaps some of the Lessers could be of help."

"Adonai, you saw them break when Satan took his last form," countered Ikanos. "The Dragon broke their spirits as well as their faith. They will not help us."

I felt unsure of my place, but I felt the need to speak. "They may not answer to you, being so far above them in power and authority, yet they may answer to me."

All were silent. Shaddai, musing silently, nodded his head. *"We must try. Go now, and see how many we can use. The next attack will come shortly."* I bowed in affirmation, then, stumbling up towards the Gates, I prepared what I would say. I knew what I needed to find. I needed a leader from amongst the Lessers, and as I neared the Throne doors, I found one.

He was as fair as the others, grimy, but still touched in ethereal beauty and innocence. In his eyes, however, burned bright defiance, and he seemed embarrassed to be hiding where he was.

"What is your name, brother?"

Looking unsure how to answer, he looked me up and down, stood, and replied, "I am Gabriy'el."

"And I am Kaos. Gabriy'el, the Seven are now Six. One is wounded. If we refuse them our help they cannot protect us for much longer. We must gather the Lessers to us and give them courage to fight."

Gazing intently at me, Gabriy'el weighed his choices. He looked out onto the field, bowed his head, and looked back into my eyes. "I am only a messenger. I was never meant for things such as this."

"None of us were meant for these things, little brother. I'm not asking for what you were meant to do; I'm asking for what you *can* do."

His eyes briefly flashed with a new fire. He took a deep breath, swallowed his nervousness, and nodded his agreement. "I will not abandon my God. And neither will the rest."

"Then we must hurry. Quickly gather all who are here, and we will make ready our defenses."

Gabriy'el went to the right of the Gate as I walked off to the left. Gathering my strength, I called out, "Brothers! Brothers, hear me!"

Inquisitive faces with fearful eyes glanced up from their huddled groups, wondering who I was. With my Essence faded and my eyes dimmed, I knew I looked neither impressive nor commanding. I was depending on Gabriy'el for that.

All around, Lessers slowly stood to their feet and began stumbling towards me. "Quickly, brothers. To the Gates! Meet at the Gates. There may yet be hope!" I ran around the pillars of the Throne Room searching for anyone still left hiding. They were all too confused or scared to argue. They shakily stood before ruggedly marching down to the doors of the Throne.

I completely scouted the perimeter, coaxing those who were not too exhausted or too wounded to follow. Several, unable to move, remained behind as I quickly ran back down to the base of the Gates.

Gabriy'el was already yelling, using his Essence to propel his voice to the nearly one thousand Lessers still forming an audience around him. So few, so embarrassingly few now stood around their inexperienced and newly appointed leader. Countless brothers lay dead at the base of the mount, while countless others fled into the distant realms of creation. Our greatest hope existed in the words of this Lesser as the others stood around wondering how much more would be expected from this remnant of Heaven.

XVIII

*"Their voice goes out into all the earth, their words
to the ends of the world…"*

-Psalm 19:4-

Gabriy'el stood towering over the masses gathered around him. Eyes, hopeless and dim, studied their self-proclaimed leader, wondering if there was anything left in heaven for which to hope. Fear turned to courage, however, as Gabriy'el enflamed their fading faith.

"Brothers, I know not where this fight takes us! I know not what waits behind the sheer veil of this life! We have long praised the Lord *our* God! We have long stood in the presence of He who fulfilled us, completed us when we had need!" Around Gabriy'el, the Lessers' eyes brightened, their heads nodding in agreement. "He gave us life, he gave us Heaven, He gave us each other, He gave us Himself, when we had need!" All was silent now, the Lessers holding their breath as he continued. "Now, Sons of God, Heaven has need of *us!* Rise, *rise* with me, *rise* with the Names of our Lord God, and let us search together that which lies beyond the veil!"

Shouts bellowed and roared from these delicate throats as the Lessers prepared to become the warriors destiny demanded. Gabriy'el yelled in the front and, as he lifted his voice, he extended his right hand into the air while his Essence flashed bright, leaving behind a one-handed, double-edged blade. Small, twin fires peered from his flashing eyes as Gabriy'el stood before the others.

Swords flashed into the air all around me as my brothers followed their new leader's example. I knew, however, that swords would not help against the menace raging around the Dragon himself. Gabriy'el stepped down from his position as his brothers clapped him on the shoulder and gripped his arm in assurance. His face beamed hope to those around him. I motioned to him through the crowd and he strode quickly towards me.

"I do not yet know what role you and your followers will play in this last stand, but the Names are waiting for you. Go to them; they will know what to do."

Gabriy'el nodded, confident that whatever the Names required of him would be fulfilled by his zealous brothers. Turning with me, we hurried down the slope of the mount back to the Names.

Shaddai looked up as we approached, somberly addressing my new companion, *"We have need. Are you capable of fulfilling what I prepare to lay before you? It is a matter of heart, not skill. I will teach you what you need to know."*

Gabriy'el, not knowing what was to be asked of him, replied without hesitation. "I have over a thousand assembled and expecting my next order. You have merely to inform me of my duties, and they will be carried out."

Shaddai waited for several long moments, shot a quick glance at me as if questioning my choice, then stared deep into Gabriy'el's eyes. *"Then you will do exactly as I say. We have but moments until the next onslaught. First, you will show your troops how to make these."* Motioning with his hands, Shaddai effortlessly crafted a weapon I had never seen before. Dull all around, light, and curved, it portrayed no conceivable purpose, as far as I could imagine. *"Then, you will teach them how to use it."*

Gabriy'el looked quizzically at the weapon, confident he could craft one, but doubting whether he could ever learn to wield one. "My Lord, I know not...."

Before he could voice his concerns, Shaddai waved his hands over Gabriy'el's face. A blinding light lanced all around as the Lesser staggered back, falling to his knees as he clawed at his eyes.

"Oh, God! My eyes! My..." In an instant, Gabriy'el grew silent and removed his hands from his eyes. His face turned from pain to wonder as he realized what Shaddai accomplished. "I know how to use them, Lord. I—will it work?"

Shaddai only nodded. *"You may commence, young one."*

Gabriy'el left stunned. His vision seemed to steadily return as his pace became straight and determined. I watched him go until he became ringed by his small force. I turned quizzically to Shaddai, hoping for more clarification.

"We needed a way to strike at them from afar. This will accomplish that goal, but I fear Gabriy'el and his remnant are too few to help turn the tide. Satan's Legions are innumerable. The Names can hold, but with Kurios wounded and Elohim lost, it is merely a matter of time." He briefly chuckled after what he said, while I turned to him, surprised and looking to him for an explanation.

"Pay me no heed, little brother. I sometimes laugh at the inevitability of our purpose. It seems as if each infinitesimal detail of our existence was planned, set out, designed for a story we cannot help but tell." He grinned, but it quickly disappeared as his face grew sober once again. *"It is as it should be. I am thankful for the story, if nothing else. At least there is always the story."*

The other Names watched Shaddai, awaiting his next action. His eyes lifted, turning to us all. *"As the enemy approaches, the Lessers will initiate their given instructions. As the Fallen come upon us, their entry point will narrow, leaving them the sky. We must stop them on both fronts."* I glanced at the bottleneck, noting its narrow passage, but curious as to how only six could hold back any sizable force. With the Names, however, there was always hope.

"Adonai, Ikanos, and Kurios will take the ground; Jireh, Je-Hoshua, and I will take the sky. Let nothing break through. They mean to not only destroy us, but the Throne as well. This is our stand, Brothers. Here our Essence shall be spilt, and only when I am broken will I cease to serve the Father and His Word." His eyes panned each face now gazing intently back towards the hope he offered before he spoke the question of a lost friend. *"Where will you stand?"*

Closing my eyes, I lowered my head, knowing this was our end. Glancing at my tattered robe convinced me I could not go down in disgrace. Concentrating for several moments, I focused on summoning up my Essence, knowing I needed armor for this last battle. My knees buckled as I worked, forcing me to catch myself with my open palms. I pitched forward, the ground rushed up to meet me. The Names glanced over at me, but before they could help me, my back arched and my mouth shot open in a silent scream. Light-coated armor encrusted itself around me, beaming off a reflective sheen. My hair grew down to my shoulders as my eyes once again burned with vengeance. Any Essence I regained was lost as I readied this last stand.

XIX

"For our struggle is not against flesh and blood, but against the rulers, against the authorities, against the powers of this dark world and against the spiritual forces of evil in the heavenly realms.

-Ephesians 6:12-

The Six stood, Kurios working out the soreness in his arm. Down the slope the Legions began to muster. My wings arched and throbbed with the remnant of my Essence. All my power crackled in my fists as I shaped my new blade. Short, with a broad base and double-edged, it shimmered white while blue and green flashes shone over its edges.

Shaddai walked a short ways down the incline, the rest of us following. *"The Lessers will hold the initial rush; we must inflict as much damage as possible. Our defense rests in our ability to break their spirit. To do so we will shatter their officers, along with the Dragon, and the others will follow suit. Remember whose you are."*

As Shaddai finished, his shield deteriorated, melding into his arm. His face flared bright as he faced the stirring army. The remaining Names took positions off to his left and right. I remained a short distance behind, not far from where the Lessers positioned themselves.

"K... kaos..."

I spun my head to glance at my feet, where Miyka'el now laid. His eyes fluttered in their newly found consciousness, but they glowed with a fierce purpose. "Miyka'el? Miyka'el!? Can you hear me?"

"Do not fight…"

Confused, I lowered myself to Miyka'el's trembling face. "Don't fight? But Miyka'el, I no longer have a choice."

"Do not fight until—you know."

"Know? Know what? Miyka'el?"

"Until you know—whose you are."

"Miyka'el, I do not know what you expect of me? Tell me! I will do anything." I glanced askance at my still, cold friend. *Anything.*

Slowly, and ever so weakly, a small smile slid across Miyka'el's face. *"It all makes sense, now."*

"Sense? Nothing makes sense anymore," I sighed to myself.

"What you—what He said; it all makes sense." With that, Miyka'el wheezed as trace amounts of Essence leaked from his mouth. I wiped away the liquid running down his chin as his eyes slid shut in exhaustion.

Sighing, I closed my eyes while kneeling over my sleeping leader. "Sleep, Miyka'el. Perhaps this will all have passed when you wake again." I quickly rose and hovered over to where Shaddai waited.

"How much longer?" I asked.

"Watch."

I looked down into the demons, their cries growing louder and louder. Something was happening, but I could not see what was causing them to cheer and howl as they were.

"Satan's doing something. Look at him, there." Pointing, Shaddai indicated where Satan hunched, his head low to the ground. "He's been like that since Gabriy'el left, if not longer. Whatever he plans, it will happen soon."

The cries and jeers exploded into a cacophonous climax before Satan's wings shot out to either side of him. Fiery jets of Dragon's breath launched deep into the sky. A beastly howl reached us where we stood. Satan surged into the sky as his armies rushed forward.

"The Dragon flies!"

Shaddai's shout shocked me from my trance. Satan flashed through the sky. Shaddai's hands flashed out in front. Wrists touching, hands closed in fists, he screamed and bellowed at the Accuser. As his roar reached his peak, a double-bladed sword with a long grip between the two blades sprang outwards to his right and left. The weapon looked as if Shaddai adjoined two swords at the base of their hilts. Unknown words riddled the blades, carved in runes I could neither read nor spell. And on the Dragon came.

"Brothers! Stand! Now, and on into judgment!" Satan came down, flames arching into Shaddai's unmoving form. To the left, the Names looked on in concern as Shaddai stood unmoving before the might of Heaven's Greatest Archangel.

Before Satan alighted he released something from within his bulging claws. Somersaulting, the form grew larger as it barreled towards Shaddai, who still stood motionless. Satan veered to the right, his wings catching the air and hurling him back to his approaching army. The hurling object elongated until we could see its two legs and arms. As it crashed to the earth, I felt my arms quiver in my armor as I looked again into that twisting mass of darkness the creature called a face.

Apollyon.

"I told you. I would come, Shaddai."

The Five around Shaddai looked on, before glancing back to the approaching Legions. They stood poised, wondering what needed to be done. Shaddai must have sensed their concern.

"Brothers, hold back the line, and seek out their leaders. Kaos, you are my rear guard. This is my fight."

"But Lord, the Legions," Adonai warned. "We cannot hold them back from you, and Kaos is weak."

"*Help will come from the least of these. You have your orders. This one is mine.*"

Apollyon's face contorted in what could have been a smile as he choked words through his own filth, "*This will be fun... little angel. Hahaheheh.*"

Slime slid from Apollyon's mouth as he reached forward with both hands, each pulsing with sheer darkness hiding his palms and his arms. Slowly, the darkness coalesced to form two gigantic weapons, each possessing long, curved blades attached to a thick shaft. *Axes.* Apollyon formed two gigantic axes, each burning with a faint, violet glow.

I looked past this craft of Satan to see all of the Legions soaring up the ascent to the Gates. The Names looked on in grim determination as our enemies came nearer. Wings flapping, claws scraping, spit drooling, eyes rolling, they came flooding unto the base of the Throne. This was the end.

The first rank of demons stumbled and fell, all screaming as they tripped up those behind them. The third and fourth rank merely alighted to fly over the ones on the ground, but before they could land, slender objects slammed them from the sky. Many of those in the front ranks never moved, but a few stumbled to their feet, clutching at small shafts protruding from their chests, legs, arms, and wings. I had no idea what I was seeing. Where were they coming from? Then I heard them.

Still stunned, I heard a familiar voice behind me. *Gabriy'el.* "To the fly, brothers! Arrows... loose!" Air whistled as the shafts launched from the same weapon Shaddai held earlier, except now every Lesser wielded an exact copy. They were the same weapons Shaddai showed Gabriy'el. The projectiles buried themselves in those charging the mount, screams tearing from their throats as Gabriy'el's arrows punctured armor and skin alike.

The Lessers took up an elevated position, continually firing down upon the encroaching army. I met Gabriy'el's eyes for the briefest moment as he gave me a smile of confidence and notched another arrow. My hopes did not last long, however, for no matter how many arrows fell into those troops, they still came on. Eventually, many of the Legion's troops formed shields of their own, or simply picked up the bodies of their fellow traitors and used them for cover.

A step, another step, one step closer, they marched in under the steady hail of projectiles. Essence wet the path to the Throne as the demons took to their wings in hopes of simply overwhelming the Lessers. Once they did the Names immediately launched into the sky, tearing apart the Enemy as they all swarmed towards the Gates.

Chaos reigned all around as Apollyon dripped venom and glared hate into the face of El Shaddai. Madness gripped his lightless eyes as Essence dripped trickled over his clear armor. The two axes slowly raised, each of the blades rubbing the other while accompanied by a sick, threatening screech.

"Why are you here, demon? You cannot mean to breach the Throne. Your end is nigh; I swear it."

"What makes you think… I came for the Father? Hahehe… ha-haha! I came for… only one thing."

"And that would be?"

"The Son. He shall be—mine, after I feast on your own, bright flesh!"

Shaddai's eyes widened in shock. I believed it to be my imagination, but it seemed Shaddai's skin grew dim. *"You speak nonsense, Fallen. There is no son, save you, and that shall shortly change."*

"Oh… come now, slave. You think… the Great Lord, the Great Dragon… knows not what you know? Fool! Perhaps now… you believe our promises."

I could not understand what either of the two was talking about, but I heard enough to know that Apollyon was never supposed to know what he told Shaddai, whose face now drooped over the curved, double-bladed sword he held humbly at his side. Secrets long untold now stood ready to be exposed. I seemed to be the only one who remained ignorant of what transpired between the forces at work.

"*Lift… your head, little angel. I have… work to do.*"

Shaddai's eyes flashed open as blue light singed the ground upon which he stood. The blades flared to life as fire and Essence swirled over the twin swords. "Your *work* ends here, Son of the Devil."

"*You choose… death. How interesting. Dying for one… who knows not what he was, or… what he was made to be.*" Apollyon's words wheezed from his mouth as dark Essence dripped from his slurping tongue. "*And after you die, Shaddai… so shall he.*" One of the axes leveled in my direction, violet light solidifying into drops of acidic Essence falling to the earth, eating away at the ground itself.

Shaddai's eyes followed the direction of the axe before they fell on me. His look turned sad, but only for an instant before fire erupted from his face, flames shimmering along his shoulders and wings. Blinding light erupted from his face, forcing me to turn away, yet as I did I heard Shaddai shout one last question over the roar of his own fire, "*What do you know of hell, demon!?*"

Apollyon managed a growl before Shaddai was upon him. One of the blades fell on the demon's hastily raised axes, even as one of the Name's wings slammed into the traitor's legs, flipping him backwards. Apollyon lurched one of his axes into the ground, anchoring him as he somersaulted to his feet.

Reddish, violet Essence leaped from Apollyon's outstretched hand after he released the embedded axe. Shaddai hastily encircled himself with his wings. A sick, burning sound erupted from them. I cringed as I heard his cry from behind his six, feathered shields, but, just as the Essence died away, the wings flew apart, Shaddai erupting from within them in fury and wrath.

Apollyon's face could not be interpreted, but his posture registered surprise as the Name fell upon him for a second time. Blades flew, axes flashed as lightning and sparks crashed from the conflicting weapons. I could barely follow their movements, but it seemed a stalemate. Neither opponent gave ground; screams and explosions rose up from the fight.

Focused on them, I temporarily forgot my role as sentry. My face glowed weakly, but I spun my head, glancing around for any sign of interference. The other Names clashed with the entire might of the Legions while the Lessers rained continuous death on those behind the first ranks as well as the few attempting to take flight and invade from above. Nothing broke through for the time being, but the Dragon remained unmoving towards the rear of his army. If he became involved I wondered if even the Names united could stand against him, especially seeing as they were distracted by the masses they currently battled.

The crashes coming from Shaddai's fight drew my gaze me as I turned again to watch their struggle. *"Can you feel it… little guardian. The end… it comes… so soon. Hahahaha!"*

Shaddai did not speak; he immediately rushed one end of his weapon towards Apollyon's right, forcing the demon to block with an axe. Shaddai then jerked his blade back towards Apollyon's left, flinging the monster's other axe wide. With both axes stretched to the sides for an instant, Shaddai hastily lunged his first blade deep into the foot of Apollyon, leaving both of his sides exposed to the demon's axes. The Enemy screamed in pain even as both of his weapons swung back in towards Shaddai, who simply stepped toward the creature and caught both arms with his hands. Holding the axes wide, Shaddai breathed into Apollyon's face, as boiling, burning Essence flashed from his eyes, boring deep into Apollyon's face. Unable to stumble back, the demon could only scream as Essence sizzled from his insides then down his face and chest.

Ceasing his blast, Shaddai grabbed his sword as he hastily jumped back, freeing the demon to fall towards the ground. Liquid seeped from Apollyon's foot as more gushed from his battered face. Shaddai managed a small smile, watching the huge figure before him crash into the ground. He sighed in relief as he turned towards me, shoulders drooped in exhaustion.

"Well, it seems this enemy will no longer serve against our God," Shaddai assured me.

Thankful for Shaddai's victory, I began approaching him, but my eyes grew wide with fear and Shaddai noticed.

Behind him, the demon's limp form twitched and pulsed, Essence still falling from his gaping wounds. Jerkily, the body lurched into the air while his feet remained on the ground. Wounds gaping and open, face disfigured and burned, armor wet and soiled, Apollyon rose up, and turned towards us both.

"So... it seems I will make you scream... before I kill you, little warrior. And then... he will scream as well..."

Shaddai's shoulders reared up; he looked amazed his foe still stood. Before either of us could move, Apollyon rushed towards Shaddai. Axes fell on the Name's swords, spittle and gore flew into the angel's face as the Name struggled to hold back the Enemy.

"Believe, Shaddai. Feel... and believe. He will... die."

Surprise turned to anger on Shaddai's face; flames leaped over his hardened wings. Apollyon's hands rose into the air, both axes crashed together, and in an instant, coalesced into one gigantic, two-handed axe. The weapon held two, curved edges, both ringed in a twisted, dark glow. One of these fell hard and sharp upon Shaddai's upraised blades.

The unthinkable flashed before my eyes as the twin-bladed weapon broke in two. My hope felt as if it died in my chest while the demon's weapon, only slightly deterred from the impact, fell through to slash deep into Shaddai's armor. Roaring in pain and rage, Shaddai took up both swords and, dual-wielding, plunged each into the exposed shoulders of his Enemy. Apollyon bellowed as he fell back from the blades.

"Is that it, demon? I need no blade to best you!"

Apollyon's arms hung limp from the recent wounds, his entire body a mesh of Essence and gore. *"Do you think... even my death will stop... him!? The dragon... comes, Shaddai. He is at your door! See... believe... you cannot... stop us!"*

With a last scream, filth sprayed upon the ground as Apollyon choked on his words. The demon raised up his weapon, and came at Shaddai. Fire and light burned from his hateful shaping as it extended above his head, preparing to crash down upon his wounded enemy. The Name, slowed by his wound, still glared with power at the approaching monster, a sword in each hand.

Just as Apollyon screamed one last time, with his axe held peaked above his head, Shaddai quickly stretched his right sword behind him, then hurled it towards the demon. Apollyon, holding his huge weapon, could neither stop nor slow. The blade buried itself hilt deep into the monster's neck, spraying Essence and bubbling liquid high into the air.

In shock, I watched as the blade slowed him, but did not kill him. A step, another step, he came on, axe still held high. Shaddai's eyes gaped wide, but he held fast to his last sword. Gurgling, the demon came closer. As Apollyon prepared to slash down with his axe, Shaddai roared in righteous hate while his wings lurched into action. He rushed towards Apollyon, grabbing the hilt still buried deep in the creature's neck, before launching into the sky. The demon slurped and spit as he ascended higher, his axe falling limp at his side.

With his other sword, Shaddai quickly sliced off the hand still clutching the axe, which fell only a few seconds before dissipating into nothingness. Shaddai carried him still higher, his wings leaving smoke trails high in the sky. Pivoting in the heavens, he turned again towards the ground, poising his sword level with Apollyon's stomach. As I watched them fall, I saw Shaddai's glowing blade dash through Apollyon's back. Down they came, with a blade through the demon's neck and torso. I could hardly watch as they streaked from on high. As they careened towards the earth, I heard a sound that made me sick. *Laughter.*

"Ha—cuk… ha… ltltltlt—hahah—koff—hahaha…" Meshed with his own gore, Apollyon laughed in Shaddai's face as he bore him towards the ground. I heard the Name scream in rage, horror, and hate as Apollyon's mutilated body slammed deep into the ground.

The explosion rippled past me as I watched Shaddai emerge from where he landed, carrying both of his Essence-stained blades. My insides felt twisted as Shaddai stalked towards me, covered in the filth of his fight.

"Is it… over, Shaddai?"

Exhausted, with drooping eyes, Shaddai only managed a weak nod. Both of us glanced around to the battle we had dangerously ignored. Then quietly, stealthily, a noise crept from the crater.

"Kaos… little cuk… glll. Kaos, do you… feel safe from Master? He will… glll cuk KOF… get you… Kaos. He always gets what he—wants."

"Ahhhhh!" Screaming, Shaddai flew into the air, a short distance above his ruined enemy. Both hands dashed out in front of him as an explosion of Essence and light flew towards the hole. Energy crackled and drilled into the ground as the foundation of heaven shook and rumbled. One last gurgling scream broke from the crater, and grew steadily quieter until it finally ceased, along with Shaddai's attack.

Hovering, I slowly approached the hole, watching Shaddai's tired form drift back towards me. Peering over the rim of the crater,

I glanced down into the deep shaft Shaddai created from his beam. Shaddai landed weaponless next to me, both swords having been absorbed for the sudden outpouring of Essence. From the shaft I heard no scream, voice, or breath. All was still.

Such was the passing of Apollyon, Son of the Dragon.

XX

"I will send my son, whom I love…"

-Luke 20:13-

With Apollyon dead I hoped the other Fallen would break and scatter, at least in the absence of the Dragon. If the Names could unite against Satan, however, we stood some chance. "We must help the others, Shaddai." Turning to him, however, I wondered if even the Lord of the Names could help us now.

His eyes were dim and dull. His skin grew dark. The fires burned low on his wings and head. Shaddai appeared spent. He weakly turned his eyes to meet mine.

"The Names… will manage, Kaos. With the Lessers helping… if Satan stays away… we may hold for yet a while longer."

Hold? Was I foolish to think of victory when the Names thought of only defense? Even Shaddai did not speak of winning this war. I glanced to the sky as arrows continued to pour into the swarm of demons mustering down near the plain. The Fallen did not halt their advance, even with Apollyon dead. They churned and rolled over their own dead as they bulged against our defenses, threatening to engulf us all the second any of the Names fell amidst the Legions.

The dead piled high while the Lessers kept launching arrows

into the Legions. "We must protect the others, Shaddai. The Names will hold back the Legions, but the Lessers can halt their advance entirely if we safeguard them."

"Kaos, only you..."

Before Shaddai could finish, screams tore into the air behind us. *Impossible. The* Legions still warred with the Names down below us. That could only mean...

"*Dragon!*" The Lessers howled and broke towards where Shaddai and I stood. A few hopeless arrows flew towards the Serpent before they shattered on his armored scales. Terror ultimately gripped them all; they came over the rise in droves. *The Lessers were broken.*

"Shaddai, we must..."

"NO! I must do this."

"You'll die, Shaddai! If Satan waits up above—we must regroup with the other Names."

Shaddai turned, sorrow gleaming in his eyes. *"What other Names?"*

I reeled, shock twisting Essence inside me into knots. I glanced down below, down where they fought–were fighting. "No, they..." I looked closer. Near the base of the Mount, far below, lightning-lanced flames sent brilliant hues of bluish-white light high above. Following the beams back to the source, I saw where the Names now stood.

Adonai's mouth moved in a battle cry, but with the distance I could hear nothing. At his feet lay Je-Hoshua, Jehovah-Jireh, and Ikanos; Essence pooling from their still faces and wet robes. *Oh, God...*

Kurios stood with his back to Adonai, each gripping a thick shaft of light which ended at a filed point of razor sharp Essence. In the off hand, both held monolithic shields with their bases jammed deep into the ground, forming a strong anchor. My glimpse of them faded as the cloud of Fallen blocking my view swarmed them again.

"I felt Ikanos die during my struggle with the Spawnling," Shaddai

interrupted. *"They will be overrun. I can feel them all, fading... one at a time. Their deaths allowed me to kill Apollyon. Otherwise, I would have lacked the rage to do so. It will soon be only us, Kaos."*

With Shaddai unable to help his brothers, and me too weak to combat the Legions, I dropped my head, remorse filling my mind, overwhelming my senses. I looked up in time to see one last explosion tear into the Fallen ranks positioned below the two Names. Kurios fell at Adonai's back; the latter must not have noticed for he neither turned nor deterred his own onslaught. At my side, however, I heard Shaddai's breath hiss as he felt another of his own perish at the hands of traitors.

The Dragon's roars turned my attention back to the Palace above. It was only a momentary distraction, long enough, however, for me to turn back in time to see a lightless blade jammed through the chest of Adonai. Surprise, mingled with pain, appeared in the Name's eyes. The look quickly turned to one of hatred; the Name dropped his spear, a bright sword flashing into his grip. In a rush, blasts erupted from Adonai as he turned to face his cowardly assailants. The dark blade still stuck deep into the back of the Name, yet it did not slow him. The Fallen fell in waves around him.

After a short time, the Fallen managed to drag away his shield, their own hands boiling as they touched its bright surface. With it gone, Adonai's free hand became a sphere of fire, slinging white flames into everything around him. When they finally disarmed him both hands were flaring dangerously. The demons circled above as others attacked from all sides. Their blades bit into the exposed skin, and Adonai's attack began to slow. As they jumped upon him, their weight bearing him down, a scream tore itself up to me, allowing me to hear his last cry.

"Immanuel!"

The Fallen dragged him to the ground, stabbing at him, clawing at him. The Essence ran thick on the ground as the demons regrouped where our champions fell. *Immanuel?* A new word, yet an old word. It felt as if I should know what it meant, but I did not. I could not reason why it would be the very last thing for the dying Name to cry. The dying Name, the next to last, now left Heaven with two weakened fighters and a band of broken Lessers.

Not again. My mind spun; I glanced down below, where the masses of the Fallen gathered. I understood. They were not regrouping; they gloated over the bodies of their stricken adversaries. Without warning the Legions suddenly began marching up the mount. It was true then. With the Lessers routed there was nothing left to hold back the Legions. All was lost. *Lost.* I turned to Shaddai, hoping for answers, before a roar pierced my ears.

My armor pulsed as terror flew with the Fallen Lord, who now glided overhead, close enough for me to feel the heat of his scorching breath. *The Dragon.* Flames preceded him for a few instants as Satan crested the rise above us, Essence staining his searing hot jaws. Teeth covered in gore and the remains of the Lessers gnashed while he landed in front of Shaddai and I. My knees buckled and my wings fluttered in fear as I dropped my pathetic, little sword.

I stumbled back, tripping over the tips of my drooping wings. Shaddai, however, lowered his head, and slowly stepped forward. Satan roared in his face as flames circled his lone enemy.

There were no words, only wrath stoking the Dragon's internal furnace. Fleshy wings shook and writhed in the air as the beast's tail crashed into the earth, sending shockwaves out into its immediate vicinity. The last of the Lessers broke past us, all of them scattering into the sky as they saw the Legions still approaching from below. We were now alone.

"So, former prince, it ends as this…" Shaddai sighed as his right hand rose slowly into the air, a short sword with a curved tip forming in his closed grip. Shaddai staggered closer; Satan snorted in contempt.

The Name came closer, sword raised in front of his eyes. Satan arced up, his wings beating towards his smaller adversary. Shaddai would have flown backwards, but Satan slowed his wings just as Shaddai began to lift off his feet, allowing Satan to rocket over him with an outstretched claw, slamming Shaddai into the earth.

Essence poured from his mouth as Shaddai slowly raised himself up, directly beneath Satan's titanic girth. Flames fell down upon him, just as dim, blue energy fell over the angel, temporarily shielding him from the flame. The fires died and the shield faded as Shaddai's eyes glazed over and he fell into the dirt.

Then Satan snorted contemptuously as he lowered his gaping maw over his limp enemy. But as his jaw came closer, Shaddai's small blade whipped up, jamming deep into the Dragon's scaly throat. Satan howled in rage. Eyes flashing hate, his claw slammed into Shaddai's legs, his teeth streaking towards the Name's face.

Just as the jaws closed over Shaddai's still frame, his eyes flew open, shooting piercing beams deep into the Dragon's burnished armor. A roar bellowed over Heaven as the last of the Names took his stand before the Father of Lies.

"*I am... El Shaddai, Serpent. You war for pride. You war for power. You war for murder, and pain, and death. In all this you warred with angels; now... you will war with me.*"

The Dragon spoke not a word. Menace dripped from his small wounds. Saliva leaked out from between monstrous fangs. Yellow, serpentine eyes narrowed as their elongated irises focused in on one stubborn, lonely figure.

"*I am of the Mel'akim. Messenger of God, Hand of the Almighty, Eye of the Spirit, a Prince of the Fiery Stones, Lord of all Shekinah, Ruler in Zion, and Bearer of the Lamp stands. I sculpt the Future, walk the Past, and elude the Present. I am with all things for He is in all things. As He is, so I am. He is El Shaddai, as am I.*"

Words silenced as the Dragon lurched forward, leathery wings and muscled talons tearing towards their enemy

"Nooo!" My weak screams died in the air along with my pathetic blasts of Essence aimed at the Dragon's eyes. On he came, all things evil portrayed in his gaze as he bore down on the last Prince. Shaddai closed his eyes for a fleeting moment; he seemed to waver on unsteady feet. In my distraction, I failed to notice the Fallen encircling behind me, nor the Serpent who now stealthily shifted course towards me instead. Before Satan came closer, however, I saw his approach. Turning to flee back towards the Steps, I ran headlong into a barricade of pikes and spears, raised by the Fallen who alighted behind me.

A shout began in my throat as I shifted backwards, hoping to elude the Dragon who I knew to be bearing down behind me. Suddenly, the faces from whom I fled vanished in a bright flash. I paused, ducking to the ground as a thunderous crash exploded above me. Satan's jaws missed, but he opened them again as his thick legs thundered closer.

I ran up towards the Steps. The loud snap of the Dragon's teeth followed close behind, the thunder of his steps rumbling closer with each step. Without warning, another explosion bit into the ground behind me. I turned mid-stride to see Shaddai. Unmoving, he stared down the Serpent, who glared past him and stared straight at me.

"Run, Kaos. Run!"

The words seemed a whisper as I hesitantly turned, leaving Shaddai behind. It turned bright all around me before I crested the lowest of the Palace steps. I lowered myself as I peered around, searching for any of the Fallen. All of them seemed to be down below, not far from where Shaddai landed. *Shaddai.*

Luminous wings arched to either side of him as his eyes glowed dangerously. A long, slim, curving sword appeared in his hands.

The Dragon stared down ponderingly before he crashed forward. Essence rang as the sword struck the creature's claws. *He will die as well.* The battle did not last long. The blade could not pierce the thick armor, and any Essence only made the fiery scales burn brighter than before. Yet Shaddai fought on.

I do not remember breathing, or thinking, when I saw him fall. The delicate wings simply folded as the Essence wrought blade clanged into the stone before it vanished into nothingness. The lone Name looked dim and distant. His still form rested in the dirt as the Dragon approached.

The last of the *Mel'akim* did not scream as Satan bit into his torso, hot Essence seeping out of Satan's mouth, dripping down to the dust below. I kneeled, falling into the dirt, watching as the last of the Names died defying the Dragon.

Tears stained my cheeks as the thunder of the Legions came up the slope; the Dragon's throat bulged as he gorged on a Name of the Most High. My sword fell from my hand onto the ground as my wings dipped and brushed the dust around me. I felt my Essence leaving me. My power faded along with my hope, along with my faith.

The Dragon finished and lazily turned towards me. He knew I had nowhere to run. Slit pupils stretched and pulsed as they looked at me. Wings rushed outwards while his thunderous claws fell closer and he came near me.

His snarls grew into words as I listened. *"Did you think you could run, little one? He has abandoned you, just as I promised. And now, you will suffer, and die."*

No longer caring, I questioned the beast. "Who abandoned me? Do you even know? You claim so much, but for all your schemes, you still need me dead. Why is that, Dragon? What do you fear in me? I am alone! Yet you hunt me! You know nothing." *We were all Lost.* "As do I."

Satan merely rolled his eyes. *"Then, in ignorance, little angel—perish."*

The head snapped back, ready to strike as I lowered my closed eyes, waiting to feel those giant teeth gash and chew into my faded frame. Yet the strike never came, and the scream I heard came not from my dying lips, but from the Second of Heaven, roaring high above me.

Glancing up, I saw what made the Dragon scream. Protruding from his broad, scaled neck, a tri-barbed spear extended. Essence dripped from the wound, but the hole through which the spear stuck soon widened, like a fire slowly spreading. The roars of the Dragon turned to cries of terror and panic as the wound widened. Claws tore at the spear, desperately trying to tear it loose.

The beast's wails turned from roars to pleas as the Dragon began to change. Unable to get the spear from his neck, the creature shrank, scales falling from his proud form. Flames coughed and wheezed into the air, while other flames burned from the wound itself. The figure became smaller and smaller, until an angel-sized figure sprawled before me, gasping for air.

Dumbstruck, I glanced behind the humbled Enemy, seeing the cause of my salvation. There, standing right where I had left him, stood Miyka'el. Burning orbs replaced his eyes, allowing tall fires to spread over his flaring face. His face looked exhausted, but his eyes burned in determination as his wings stood wide and bright behind him.

Cautiously glancing at Satan, I stumbled towards my Captain. "Did you… did you…?"

"I'm not sure. We will see. I have rested for far too long. Shaddai's death tore me from my daze. I watched… *that*… blaspheme a Name of God. As soon as he was distracted with you, I threw all my Essence into that spear, and hurled it towards his head. I missed."

"I do not think it would have mattered, Miyka'el. Shaddai

barely managed to finish Apollyon. As Satan is stronger, we will have no chance if your blow did not destroy him."

"The Legions are still coming; the Throne is undefended.

"The Dragon's arrival broke Gabriy'el and his forces." I gazed despairingly to the earth. "We are the last ones."

Miyka'el slowly nodded in acceptance, glancing from the Legions to the Gates of the Throne. As he turned back to me, his eyes widened. I spun in time to see Miyka'el's same spear spiraling through the air towards my Captain's chest. Timeless instants seemed to slow as I launched in front of Miyka'el, spinning him to my right and covering him with my wings.

My eyes closed and my mouth clenched as I waited. The moment lasted an eternity, and then pain exploded into my side. I gasped into my Captain's ear as I heard him scream.

I fell backwards, the shaft clanging into the ground as the head reverberated within me. My vision dimmed, blurred, and went dark. Essence poured from my wound. I remember my hands feeling wet. And as I drifted away, the last I heard was Satan's laughs while Miyka'el clasped my limp head to his quivering chest.

Then all grew silent. And I began to remember…

> *"Kaos, you know what this will mean."*
> *Voices—a strange voice, but one I knew.*
> *"They will hate you."*
> *I knew that; I knew something else.*
> *"They will despise you."*
> *Yes—I know.*
> *"This is only the beginning."*
> *How long will it last?*
> *"There will be others. Others I will bring."*
> *Will it hurt?*
> *Silence. "Yes. It will hurt."*

Why them? Why now?

"Because, I love them."

I love you, too.

Silence again. "I know, little one. I know."

Sad. The voice… No other way?

"This is the only way. You *are* the only Way."

Will I know? Will I remember?

"No. You will be alone."

Never alone since—forever.

"Are you willing?"

I trusted the voice. I loved the voice. Yes.

"It begins soon. The Beginning."

Obedience. Necessary for them.

"I will come, soon. You will know."

The Voice. Who? Why?

"You will be their hope."

I will. I am. Why? The Others—why me?

"You are my Son. I am that I am."

Son? My name is Kaos.

"And your name shall be Immanuel."

Existing forever, before forever.

"God with Us."

My name is…

"The Son of the Most High!"

May this cup pass from me.

"His kingdom will never end."

Your Will be done.

"In the beginning was the Word."

Together.

"And the Word was with God."

Since Forever.

"And the Word was God."

I am that I am.
"Yes, my Son. You are."

The eyes of the dead Kaos sprang open. Miyka'el's sobs grew silent as he stared down into the one he held. Eyes white with holy fire burned pure and fierce. Slowly, the One stood. A short distance away, a creature once beautiful, ceased its laughter.

Wings broke off and fell from the One's back. Armor shattered and dropped away. The one named Miyka'el staggered back, falling to his knees, his wings flew over his face as he cowered in the earth. The being once named for his beauty growled and snarled at the One who was risen. A spear still pierced his side. Slowly, a hand lowered and grasped the spear; it melted into nothing.

"Who are you, Lesser!? You think your tricks can break the new Lord of Heaven!?" Behind the Accuser, Legions approached, all of them coated in perverse power. They came closer, yet the One did not move.

The other grew confident, surrounded by his troops. "Who are you, little brother? You will die here, but I long to know your name."

The One's eyes slid shut then opened, riveting on the Accuser. *"I Am Immanuel."*

A twitch of fear flashed across the face of the Accuser as an evil, dark blade formed in his hand. "Lies! No one bears that name! I am here to claim that title from the one who hides on his white-washed throne."

The army behind surged forward, past their Lord. Then the One named Immanuel spoke.

"Tetelestai." It is finished.

The army stopped, glancing around, unsure of the strange tongue. Then a faint noise, quiet, then growing louder, spread through the Legions. Cracking, and snapping, associated with frantic screams came flying towards the One and his Accuser.

From far in the rear, thousands of the hosts were falling on their faces. As the wave of the fallen reached the forward ranks, they saw what brought the Fallen to the ground. All around the One, the knees of the rebels snapped and broke. Not a single traitor in the countless Legions remained standing. Every knee was bent; every head was bowed.

The one known as Satan turned about, terror gripping his core as his armies bowed down before the One. The screams intensified as the Legions realized their Essence could not be used to fix what was done. While the armies of the damned praised Him with their screams, Immanuel raised his eyes to Satan and slowly approached the trembling Prince.

XXI

"I saw Satan fall like lightning from heaven."

-Luke 10:18-

All around the Legions moaned in agony, clutching at their shattered legs. The former Dragon glared with hatred at Immanuel. His teeth, clamped together, gnashed and grinded as the One walked closer. His dark blade waved menacingly in his shaking hand. "I am Lord… of the Hosts!" His feeble cry did nothing to slow the approach of his judgment.

Each step brought the One closer, and each one shriveled the Enemy that much more. Whimpering, the former Prince, the Dragon, the Voice of the Legions, quivered at the feet of Immanuel. Satan glared up into the eyes of the One, standing over him.

Suddenly, the blade snaked up from Satan's hand, flying towards the face of the One. Before the sword fell, a shining hand caught it, flicking the blade aside. Enraged, the Accuser arose, striking again, and again. With each strike, the traitor flung charge after charge into the face of the One, while Immanuel merely brushed strike after strike aside.

"He meant to betray us!"

"He meant to love you."

"He's replacing us!"

"*You are irreplaceable.*"

"He only loves Himself."

"*He only loves what is holy.*"

"Then how can He ever love *me!?*"

"*By making you perfect.*"

"He makes nothing perfect!"

"*He waits.*"

"For what?"

"*Me.*"

"You? What can you do, Lesser?!"

"*Love.*"

"What makes you sure He loves you?"

"*Because I love myself.*"

"Madness—"

"*I Am the Son, Lucifer.*"

"That name…gone. No, only One…"

"*You assaulted the Gates of the Father.*"

"I sought to defend my brothers."

"*You blasphemed the Names of God.*"

"Servants of a witless deity."

"*You deceived the hosts of Heaven.*"

"They followed Truth."

"*Yet all this could be forgiven.*"

Satan's anger froze in his eyes. A faint gasp of hope breathed inside the traitor. For so long he considered himself doomed to bring about what had been done. Now, with victory gone, and ambitions destroyed, forgiveness became all the twisted Lord of the Hosts desired.

"*Except, you sought the unforgivable.*"

"I know your plans! I feel your sick plots. I know your dreams. You mean to begin where I ended, deceiving even the Father, to gain what I have lost."

Immanuel's eyes drooped in sadness before rising again to stare into the face of His Accuser. *"You sat at the Throne with my Father. You were woven from the fabric of untouched chaos. You stood Watch over the Ancient Stones. You paced the boundaries of Heaven before the others first breathed life. You crafted beauty in this place. Your work has been seen since God first moved. Yet through all this, you wanted to be the one thing you could never be. Me."*

Satan raised his blade one final time, to only have Immanuel grab the weapon in mid-air, stare deep into his enemy's eyes, and breathe one last promise into the traitor's face. *"Cursed are you over all Creation."*

Fire ringed Satan's face, but it was not his own. The Second of Heaven screamed as the flames spread over his armies. The Legions writhed, crying mercy, until all of Heaven was filled with wailing and gnashing of teeth. The noise rose to a final tumult as the doors behind the One once known as Kaos burst open, and from within boomed the judgment of the Father.

One last scream tore from Satan's throat before he, along with all his followers, vanished in the twinkling of an eye, allowing Heaven to fall silent once more.

XXII

"I am the resurrection and the life. He who believes
in Me will live, even though he dies."

-John 11:25-

Distant echoes of Heaven's quaking foundations rumbled over a forsaken battlefield. Gore and crusted Essence pooled and lay stagnate upon a ruined landscape while the bodies of the dead slumbered in their filth. Alone, before a vast expanse of emptiness, stood a lone figure, silhouetted against the madness of a torn paradise.

There existed no movement, no life, only a tense, taut breath hissing through clenched jaws. Power enraptured this lone figure, even as His shoulders quivered in grief. His feet singed the stones upon which He walked. Even so, His shoulders stilled as He turned once again to the Throne Room of His Father, and He saw His friend.

There, held silent in death, lay the patient, peaceful form of Novation. Dry Essence crusted over his smooth jaw and fine skin. Blank, soulless eyes peered lifelessly into the heavens, conducting a motionless search that no one should ever know.

Immanuel's feet quivered as He walked towards His lost friend. From all around, curious faces and inquisitive figures appeared, watching their Savior react to an unconquered enemy: Death.

From above, the thundering echo of untainted eternity boomed from within the walls of the Throne.

The Son paused over his friend, tears poised where they glistened in Immanuel's compassionate eyes. Light flared dangerously around his clinched fists as the sky broke overhead with explosions and chaos. All around, angels inched closer to witness the power of their Lord. Prisms of color ran through his hair before they coalesced into a brilliant halo of blinding light that settled onto his crown. Fire ringed his feet as the earth cracked at his step. In a flash, Immanuel's hands flew open, lightning leaping from his open palms, water fell from the sky, fire lurched from the earth, and wind tore through the heavens.

And He wept.

As He sobbed, clinched in His own power, He heard the Others, the Lesser Brothers.

"See how He loved him!"

"Could not this Savior, who freed us all from our doubt, have kept this brother, kept the others, from dying?"

Immanuel heard and felt their questions circulating around a cradled faith. It was time to open their eyes.

"*Did I not say to you that if you believe, you will see the glory of God?!*" His voice thundered over the very storm He created. Flaring eyes once locked onto Novation rose to the now open gates of the Throne. "*Father, I thank You that You have heard Me.*"

Lessers, quivering all around, fell away from the Son, scrambling to find cover. Before they could escape from His sight, however, a promise rang out from the Voice of their Savior.

"*Behold! I am making all things new!*" With that, Immanuel's hands reached out, both arms stretched taut against the sky. Light and fire encircled Him as explosions rent the air around Him. Liquid Essence cascaded from his wrists as screams erupted from the

throats of the Lessers. Turmoil reigned around the body of his lifeless friend until the Son spoke again.

"Novation! *Arise!*"

All of heaven fell into darkness. There was no light, no direction, no feeling, no noise. All became nothing. Then slowly, very
slowly the darkness seemed to pull itself away from the corners of
the horizon. Little by little, all of that nightmarish dark fled into
the still form of Novation, still huddled at the feet of Immanuel.
The lightless madness seeped into his little frame, until Immanuel
spoke again.

"*Well done, Little One. Awake, for you are but sleeping.*" With that,
Immanuel extended a shining hand as Novation's eyes crawled open.

First, light as green as shallow tides of the sea glowed out from
Novation's now rising head. All around him, his brothers crouched
in the dirt, staring motionless at the risen body of their friend. At
first, he seemed full of confusion, feeling this way and that making
sure he was alive. Then he remembered himself, and while turning,
came face to face with Kaos.

"Brother?"

"*At one time I was.*"

Novation spoke on, unhindered by what he did not understand.
"Satan. He…"

"*Is no longer a concern of yours.*"

"What of the things he promised, or threatened? What of Man?"

Immanuel's eyes slid shut, opening quickly and without regret.
"*I will do for them as I have done for you.*"

Immanuel merely turned and walked out towards the now
vacant Plain of Heaven. His steps carried Him slowly into the field
around the Throne. The Brothers watched Him go, all of them
silent. Novation bowed his head and peered off with the rest.

From the open doors of the Throne came the Father's Voice,

nearly shattering the very existence of Heaven. Immanuel answered as the Word of God.

"In the beginning was the Word."

"And the Word was with God."

"And the Word was God."

"He was with God in the beginning."

"All things came into being through Him."

"So shall it be."

"Come; let us make Man in our image."

"It is Time."

"The genesis of things."

"Of all things."

"Our will be done."

"Not my will, but yours be done."

Light flashed white through the foundations of time and space. And behold, all was good.

EPILOGUE

"I will display my glory among the nations, and all the nations will
see the punishment I inflict and the hand I lay upon them."

-Ezekiel 39:21-

Such was the coming of the Son in Heaven. Silence reigned in that place as the scattered gathered to hear the previously quiet voice of their God. Fear was replaced with hope, doubt by faith, and despair by love. He who was Kaos, self-sustained since before the beginning, remembered.

Promises were made, and as the servants of the Most High wept for those lost, prophecies were penned for events yet to come. Soon after, history began, as God sculpted that which Satan feared through Immanuel Himself. Man was born, and with Him the incarnation of God's plan.

There remain questions left unanswered. The dead remain poised in between, groaning in eager expectation for something yet to come. The Father's plan crafted Time itself in preparation for the unfolding of His Glory. The ways yet to come remain dark to all, except to the Father. For to Him, darkness must shine as the light.

As for Kaos, he wept for the lost, for the path he had yet to walk. Pain is necessary in existence, and for the One who bears the wrath of Heaven there can be no greater pain.

Stories left untold in these recollections still occur in a Time to come, yet the revelation of the future remains solely in the hands of the Word Himself. The War in Heaven, the sacrifices of the least, and the path made clear by the death of a Son, will remain forever bound within the memories of Kaos.